Isabel of the *Whales*

Isabel
of the
Whales

Hester Velmans

SCHOLASTIC INC.
New York Toronto London Auckland Sydney
Mexico City New Delhi Hong Kong Buenos Aires

ISBN-13: 978-0-439-93282-0
ISBN-10: 0-439-93282-3

Text copyright © 2005 by Hester Velmans.
Cover illustration copyright © 2005 by Jesse Reisch. Interior whale illustration copyright © 2005 by Lars Hokanson. All rights reserved. Published by Scholastic Inc., 557 Broadway, New York, NY 10012, by arrangement with Random House Children's Books, a division of Random House, Inc. SCHOLASTIC and associated logos are trademarks and/or registered trademarks of Scholastic Inc.

Lines from "The Love Song of J. Alfred Prufrock," from *Prufrock and Other Observations*, by T. S. Eliot, reprinted with the permission of Faber and Faber Ltd.

Material from *Carl Sagan's Cosmic Connection: An Extraterrestrial Perspective*, by Carl Sagan and Jerome Agel, reprinted with the permission of Cambridge University Press.

12 11 10 9 8 7 6 5 4 3 2 1   7 8 9 10 11 12/0

Printed in the U.S.A.   40

First Scholastic printing, March 2007

The text of this book is set in 12-point Adobe Caslon Regular.

Book design by Angela Carlino

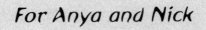

For Anya and Nick

My beloved is mine, and I am his: he feedeth
  among the lilies.
Until the daybreak, and the shadows flee away.

The Song of Songs (Old Testament)

one

CALL me Isabel. That's my name, though in my family you'd never know it. Someone please tell me why, when your parents have picked out a perfectly good name for you, they then turn around and call you something totally dumb instead, like Unchkins or the Bonz or Jellyman? In my case, it was Izzy at first, when I was a baby, but as soon as I could talk it got to be Lizzie, which later turned into (thanks to my *brilliant* big brothers) the Lizard—you know, all slimy and cold, with a forked tongue.

So I was the Lizard for a while, but then my brothers decided *that* was boring, and they came up with a new name for me. Iguana. Not a cute little lizard, but a big ugly lizard. Ig for short, which rhymes with pig. By the time I was eleven, I was Iggie most of the time. Which I didn't mind as much because it wasn't so far removed from Izzy, or Isabel.

We live just outside Provincetown, at the tip of Cape Cod. Our house is a shingled Victorian that at one time or another has been painted all these different shades of blue. It has a wide front porch, a narrow back porch, and lots of rooms all opening up into each other, which is great for hide-and-seek. My room is the smallest room in the house. It's on the third floor and what's special about it is that it has a three-sided window inside a small turret stuck onto the side of the roof—like a tower for a princess. It has a window seat, and if you lift out the screen you can climb onto the roof and have a great view of all the backyards on our street. On a clear day, you can see the sea. Even though I don't have my own bathroom up there, I wouldn't want to change rooms with any other kid in the world. That year I had a rainbow-colored sign on my door that read:

1. KNOCK
2. Do Not Enter
3. Girls Only Allowed
4. And I mean it!

On a Saturday at the end of May, Kristen and Molly came over to my house. The three of us have been best friends since kindergarten. I don't remember who first came up with the idea, but somehow we decided on a game of

Truth or Dare. We lay sprawled on my bed, staring up at the ceiling.

Since it was my house, it was my turn to ask first. "Okay, Molly!" I said.

"Me?" said Molly, already in a giggly mood.

"Yes, you. Ms. Molly Masterson. Tell us . . . please tell us who you *like*."

"Who I like?" asked Molly, playing dumb. "Well, I like Kristen, I guess, and I like you . . ."

"Which *boy* you like," said Kristen patiently.

Anyone with eyes in their head could see that Molly liked my middle brother Jacob. She was always trying to get us to bake cookies or something because that way we'd be downstairs, in the kitchen, where we might bump into him. When we did, she would start playing with her pale curly hair, twirling it around her fingers or folding it into a bun, as if she were a model posing for a magazine cover. I had even caught her throwing a sultry glance or two in Jacob's direction, with this silly coy expression on her face. It was kind of pathetic. Jacob totally ignored her, of course—my brothers always ignored my friends—but from the way he strutted when she was around, you could tell he'd noticed, all right. Molly really annoyed me sometimes, even though she was my best friend. I hated it when she put on that silly-little-blonde act. It made me feel like such a big brown lump, compared to her.

"I don't like anyone!" she squealed now, pulling at her hair and twisting it into a ponytail.

"Are you *sure*?" I wheedled.

"Of course I'm sure!"

"Ohh-kay," I said, sort of sarcastic. "Be like that. Fine. She refuses to tell the truth. What dare do we have for Candidate Number One?"

"Uh," Kristen said. "I can't think of anything."

"Wait," I said. "I know! Molly has to go downstairs, sneak into the boys' room, and throw Jacob's pillow out the window."

"No!" screeched Molly. She was getting all red.

"Truth or dare," Kristen chanted, "truth or dare! You've got to do it, Molly!"

We had to help her, of course, to make sure the coast was clear, and I had to point out which bed was Jacob's. The pillow landed way up in the apple tree behind the back porch. I thought I was going to crack a rib, we were laughing so much, and Molly acted like she was about to faint, but in the end the whole joke sort of fizzled out, since it seemed my brothers had gone to baseball practice and they weren't around to get mad at us. I'd be the one to get it later, at bedtime, when Jacob figured out what had happened to his pillow.

"Me next," said Molly when we were back in my room. "I dare both of you to tell me—have you ever thought you were really, you know, special?"

"What do you mean, special?" I said.

"I mean, different. I mean, like, not really who you really are—living here, in Provincetown, going to Veterans Memorial School, being just, you know, ordinary."

"Oh! *I* know!" exclaimed Kristen.

"Yeah?" said Molly.

"Yeah! I used to think I was adopted," Kristen confessed. I had to pinch my nose hard to stop myself from laughing. I couldn't help it. Kristen is the fifth of six children, all redheads like her mom. You could say there's a distinct family resemblance.

Kristen glared at me. ". . . And my real parents were movie stars, they had to give me up at birth because the studio made them, you know, because it was before they got married, but then someday they're sorry for what they've done, and they decide to get me back, and they have me come and live with them in Beverly Hills, and they give me parts in their movies and everything—"

"Yeah, and like me," Molly interrupted excitedly, "I—*swear* you'll never tell anyone. . . ."

We swore.

"You know how Michael Preston spends his summers on the cape?"

"Duh," I said. Michael Preston was the lead singer of the band Grist for the Mill. I had every one of their albums. So did Molly and Kristen. I had a poster of him pinned above my goldfish bowl, next to my whale posters and marine charts. "So . . . ?" I said.

"I'm pretty sure I'm going to run into him someday, I don't know exactly how, like he sees me on the beach, or I find his dog who's run away—you know, something like that . . ." (*"I didn't know Michael Preston had a dog, did you?"* I whispered to Kristen, who giggled.) ". . . and then he discovers me, and first he'll use me, maybe, as a backup singer—"

"Or one of the dancers!" Kristen breathed. She was getting all starry-eyed, like Molly.

"But later he persuades me to go solo, and I get to be a *huge* star. And then we get married—"

"How romantic!" I broke in. "But you're forgetting something, aren't you?"

"What?" asked Molly.

"You don't really sing," I said. I'm such a realist.

"I do sing! I love to sing!"

"Yeah, lip-synching in front of your bedroom mirror," said Kristen.

"Oh yeah?" snorted Molly, tossing back her hair. "I'm going to take voice lessons. That's what I'm asking for, for my birthday."

"Voice lessons are expensive," said Kristen worriedly.

They were both looking a bit dejected, and I suddenly felt bad for Molly. "That's great," I told her. "I think that's a great idea. You never know."

"You never know," Molly agreed.

I'd always had the feeling that I was special too, but I would never, ever have told anyone. I didn't want people to think I was conceited. I mean, I knew girls like me weren't really expected to be anything special. Not big bony girls with short hair that wouldn't curl and round, plain old ordinary brown eyes.

Still, ever since I could remember, I'd been convinced I was different somehow—like I had been chosen for some great part. Like I had royal blood (though that wasn't it) or like I was going to be the first, or the youngest, or the best, or the only one to do something truly awesome. I didn't know what it was, then. It wasn't being the child of movie actors, or getting to be on MTV, or winning a beauty contest, or anything dumb like that. It was just about being singled out for something.

I wished I knew for what!

Finally it was my turn to be grilled. Molly pulled Kristen into the hall and I heard them conferring in whispers. I heard Kristen giggling, and Molly's delighted "*No!*" I braced myself, expecting to be asked something truly embarrassing.

"All right, Iggie," said Kristen, coming back in the room. "Truth or dare. What's the story with you and those whales, anyway?"

"Yeah, why are you so obsessed with them?" Molly chimed in.

"I'm *not* obsessed!" I protested. I felt myself go red. I knew my friends thought I was a little weird, but they'd never come out and said so before. Instead of collecting something cute like ponies or Beanie Babies, like most of the girls I knew, I had a whole shelf of little glass whales and dolphins in my room. I'd also amassed at least a dozen stuffed whales over the years, the largest of which was a black and white orca, by now kind of gray and bedraggled. He was called Snorkel, I'd had him forever, and I still needed him at night to fall asleep.

"You are . . . you have, what's it called, a fetish," Molly said solemnly.

"Oh, please!" I scoffed.

"Go on, fess up! Truth or dare," Kristen insisted.

"Okay," I said. "Only, I don't know what there is to explain. I just like them, that's all."

"Or, instead, we could make you do something really gross," said Kristen. "Like on *Fear Factor*. We'll find some delicious stinky bait and earthworms for you to swallow."

I shuddered. "I like whales, I guess, because they're big. . . ."

"So are elephants, and you're not stuck on elephants, are you," observed Kristen.

"Whales are much bigger than elephants, they're the biggest, most powerful living creatures on earth," I went on, "and they're, like, really intelligent. . . ."

"How do you know?" asked Molly.

"I've read up about them, that's how I know," I said. "And—they take care of their young, and they can communicate with each other in the neatest way. . . ."

Kristen yawned. Molly was leaning out the window, to see if my brothers had come home yet. "Whatever," she said. They hadn't bought my explanation, but to my relief they didn't seem too interested in digging up any worms for me to eat.

What I hadn't told them, because it was sort of private, was that when I was little my great-grandmother once told me that back in Ireland, people used to think sea mammals like seals and whales could come on land and turn into people. An ancestor of hers had married one, once. I don't know why, but I loved that story. And sometimes, in bed at night, I'd feel myself sinking into a still green ocean, and then I'd dream I was swimming with the seals, and the whales, and all the animals of the deep.

Of all the teachers I'd had, Mr. Peake, my fifth-grade teacher, was by far my favorite. Our class always seemed to put him in a great mood. He would smile when you asked him a good question or gave the right answer, as if he was saying to himself, "See? I *knew* they had it in them." By coincidence, that semester we happened to be studying marine mammals—my favorite subject, of course. Most of the girls loved the dolphins and seals, while the boys preferred the whales and manatees and killer whales. I didn't want to show off or anything, but I knew more about the subject than anyone else in the class. Every time we visited our grandparents in Boston, I'd always beg my parents to take me to the aquarium. I loved the warm, hushed, humid atmosphere of that place, the way the big and small creatures in the dusky tanks swam around as if they didn't notice they were being stared at by all those human eyes. When I was little I'd start crying when it was time to go home. My parents told me that one time, they'd had to pick me up and carry me out of there kicking and screaming.

I had already handed in my assignment—the last one of the year—even though Mr. Peake had given us a week's extension. You were supposed to write a report on how man had made a difference in the lives of marine mammals. I couldn't wait to find out what Mr. Peake thought of mine. I'd had this neat idea of telling the story of *Moby Dick* from the point of view of the great whale himself—how he'd been happy swimming around in the big ocean minding his own business until Captain Ahab came along and just kept bugging him, and how what Moby Dick did to Ahab, like biting off his leg, was only done in self-defense. And how Captain Ahab just wasted whales' lives, killing them for the sport or for the money or for ballast. And how that was what a lot of fishermen and hunters did today, too. I put in all this stuff about saving the dolphins and the whales and the oceans, because it was something close to my heart, and I knew Mr. Peake went for that sort of thing too. He really seemed to care, unlike most of the adults I knew.

"Anyone interested in going on a whale watch?" he asked us at the start of class the next Monday, in a calm, normal voice, as if it wasn't a very big deal.

It was the moment I'd been waiting for. For a moment I sat there in a happy daze. *At last!* Then I joined in the hullabaloo of kids cheering and yelling and jabbing their hands in the air, going *Woo-woo-woo!*

Mr. Peake grinned. He knew we'd been wondering when he'd make the announcement. Last year's fifth grade had gone on a whale watch just before the end of the spring semester. It was a tradition at our school. When my brothers had gone on their respective whale watches, I'd been green with envy. I remembered thinking how unfair it was—they didn't even particularly care about whales! Anyway, I knew this year it would be my turn. I'd been looking forward to it for months.

"Here are some forms for your parents to fill out," Mr. Peake said, handing out some green sheets. "You will all have to get up very early next Friday."

There was a groan from the class.

"If there are any landlubbers who prefer to sleep late, of course . . . ," he teased.

We all sat up straight and keen, as if getting up at 6 a.m. was what we did every day.

"You might want to bring a camera," he said. "And pack a lunch, and a jacket or raincoat."

"What about binoculars?" asked Kristen.

"You may bring those, too, if you wish. But it's not really necessary for watching whales. Usually, if there are any humpbacks in the area, they'll come right up to the boat."

"You mean *they* come looking for *us*?" I asked excitedly. It took Captain Ahab months to hunt down Moby Dick.

"Sit down, Isabel," said Mr. Peake. "There's no need to jump up and down like that. Well, we don't know what draws them to us, but the answer is yes. They seem to like to come over and take a good look at us."

I hadn't realized I'd been jumping up and down. I planted myself firmly in my seat and tried to get hold of myself.

"But why?" asked Jim Tilton.

"We don't know why. And that's not the only thing we don't know about whales. They are still a great mystery to us."

"Like, no one knows why they make those singing sounds," I said. I couldn't help myself.

"We can speculate, but no one knows for sure," said Mr. Peake. "You know, class, the study of whales in their own environment is a relatively new thing."

"How come?" asked Ruth.

"I guess it wasn't really considered that important. As long as we were exploiting the whale . . . what were we exploiting whales for, Isabel?" he threw out at me.

"For their blubber and their oil—oh, and I guess their

whalebone, sir?" I answered demurely. I was gripping the edge of my seat, to keep myself sitting still.

"Correct! As I was saying, as long as whales were getting killed anyway, scientists who were studying whales would wait for a dead whale to turn up, and then they'd go over and inspect the carcass. Well, there is only so much you can learn about an animal from its dead body, isn't there? There's so much more to be learned from observing it alive. But we didn't really think of that—not until it became clear that whales were going to die out, that they were threatened with . . . Jameel?"

"Extinction?" said Jameel.

"Good! Extinction. Then all of a sudden we started worrying about them, and we realized that soon it would be too late to understand them, let alone save them."

"Aren't whales still getting hunted?" asked Jason Tutorini.

"Unfortunately, there are some nations of the world that have refused to accept the guidelines of the International Whaling Commission and are still allowing some whaling."

"So they're still getting killed!" said Jason.

"They are still getting killed," sighed Mr. Peake, shaking his head. "And with modern weapons—exploding harpoons and the like."

"Tell us about the exploding harpoons!" yelled Bobby Bing, who always sat in the back of the class and didn't usually pay much attention. Except when the subject was gruesome enough.

"The whales don't stand much of a chance with those. They are harpoons equipped with a sort of grenade, which explodes a few seconds after it anchors itself in the whale's flesh. You can imagine what sort of carnage those can cause."

"Will I get seasick?" asked Corinne. She had a habit of changing the subject just when it was getting interesting.

"If the sea is very rough, we'll postpone our trip," said Mr. Peake. "And you may ask your parents to give you some medication for seasickness, if you're worried about it."

"But Mr. Peake, what if we don't get to see any whales?" complained Corinne.

"We'll be disappointed, of course," said Mr. Peake. "But Captain Segal, the captain of the ship, tells me it is very unusual not to spot at least one or two whales around these parts in the springtime. The whales are just as curious about you and me as we are about them."

The whales, curious about me! I felt this great thrill at the thought, a thrill that wormed its way from my belly to my throat and ended up tickling my nose.

"Arrr-tchoo!" I sneezed, very loudly.

Mr. Peake turned to me and smiled. "Don't get sick now, Isabel. I wouldn't want you, of all people, to miss this."

Then I knew. I was sure. He had read my whale story! And he thought it was good! He thought I was special! I was so happy I could have jumped up and given him a hug or something!

But of course I didn't. I just rubbed my nose and shrugged and pretended I had suddenly found something really interesting to read in my science textbook.

two

"Iggie, didn't you hear Mom calling you? Dinner's cooked, and it's your turn to set the table!"

"*Com*-ing," I yelled. I had just finished packing my backpack with stuff for the whale watch the next day—sunglasses, a parka, a granola bar.

"Alex?"

"What? Come on, I'm starving!"

In my socks I slid down the corridor after my brother, picking up a little too much speed and crashing into his ankles.

"Hey, watch it!" he laughed, giving me a shove backward

with his foot. I crashed to the floor and he pounced, grabbing me by the ankle so I couldn't get up.

"Can I have your camera tomorrow?" I panted, kicking him hard with the foot that was free.

"Hey, stop it!" Still laughing, he twisted my foot around so that I was forced onto my stomach. "No, why should I let *you* have *my* camera, my little iggie-pig-gie-face!" he drawled.

"*You* know. It's my whale watch tomorrow, and I don't have a camera. Please, Alex?" I begged. I had stopped kicking and just let myself go limp, which I knew from experience was the best way to make him stop.

He let go and I struggled to my feet. "Oh, the *whale watch*!" he simpered, following me into the kitchen. "Gol-*ly*! Your class going on a whale watch? Our little Iggikins, going on a whale watch. Well, well, well!" Alexander had this way of making you feel like a three-year-old. "Ah, Queequeg, me hearty. Watch out for the mad bloodthirsty whale. Blood and gore," he growled at me as I was trying to reach for the dishes, "Blo-hoh-hood and go-ho-hore!"—slobbering the words right in my face, his tongue hanging out of his mouth, his eyes popping out of his head.

"No, all I asked—Alex! All I asked," I said coolly, slamming the plates down on the table, "is, can I have your camera?"

"No, you can't have it."

"Mom! Alex says he won't let me take his camera on the whale watch!"

"I didn't say she couldn't *take* it. I said she can't *have* it. I want it back."

"All right," sighed Mom, ladling out noodles. "Stop bickering, you two. Come on Alex, you know how much this field trip means to her. She's been looking forward to it for ages. Of course you'll let her use your camera."

"I never said I wouldn't," sniffed Alex. "I'm such a *nice* big brother. I won't even cry if she drops it overboard. I'll just kill her."

"You know I won't do that!" I said indignantly. "You know I'm responsible! You know I'll take good care of it!"

"All right, all right," said Alex. "All *right*!"

"Uh-oh, Alex, you've gone and made the Ig cry again," jeered Jacob.

It was *so* unfair. I hadn't been crying. After he said it, *that's* when I felt like crying.

I didn't say another word for the rest of the meal. I picked at my food and brooded about what my brothers would say when they found out how special I was, how lucky they were to have a sister like me, destined for something really important. Someday I'd astonish them, and then they'd regret not paying more attention to me when we were kids. How they'd wish they'd been nicer to their little sister, instead of wasting their time inventing new and improved nicknames for me!

I couldn't sleep that night. I went to bed especially early, but it was no good. I kept jumping out of bed and checking the pile of clothes I'd put out on my chair, and my nylon backpack with Alexander's precious camera in it. I was still awake at midnight. I remember the lighted numbers on my alarm clock winking at me.

Then I must have slept a little, because when the alarm went off my heart was pounding, and it took me a few seconds to realize where I was. I had been having one of those half-dreams where you're sure you're awake. I kept being rocked by waves—up and down, up and down, side to side—and it was getting really annoying, because I knew I should get up and get dressed so I wouldn't miss the bus, but the more I tried to stop the rocking the faster it got, the harder the waves slapped at my skin, and the more helpless I felt.

It was a relief to realize I had only been dreaming. I got up, threw on my clothes, grabbed my lunch, yelled goodbye to my parents who were still in bed, and ran out the door when I heard Molly's car honking outside. Her dad had volunteered to get up early to drive us to school.

On the bus to the harbor I sat in a cold bleary daze. I wished I'd worn a different sweater; the one I had on was itchy around my neck. My friends were chattering, but I didn't feel like talking. My tongue was dry and my head felt empty. I just sat there like a zombie, swaying with the swerving of the bus. I kept keeling over onto Molly's shoulder.

"Stop it, Iggie!" she said, and shoved me up against the window.

"Ou-ouch," I moaned weakly.

Finally we pulled up to the dock where our ship was rocking gently against the pilings.

It was a beautiful, glimmery morning. There were zillions of clouds all lined up evenly in the sky, as if they had someplace to go. The air smelled salty, fishy, mysterious. The breeze was just stiff enough to fill your eyes and nose. You could taste it. And there were cawing seagulls all over the place, making a crazy racket. I rubbed my eyes.

The *Explorer* was not a big boat. It was sort of disappointing, actually. I had expected a *real* ship, with masts and sails and things. The *Explorer* looked like any old sightseeing boat, with white railings, a top and a bottom deck, and a middle section with long benches and rolled-up vinyl blinds that could be let down if the weather got rough. Still, I was one of the first to run up the gangway. I was suddenly wide awake and raring to go. I was going to see real live whales, somewhere out there in the ocean! I felt as if I was stepping onto a moving platform that was about to take me on the greatest ride of my life.

At first there wasn't much to see. Nothing, in fact, except for the horizon and the occasional boat. By the time we'd been out on the water more than two hours, some of the kids had started getting fidgety. I looked out at the sea, which was empty of anything but foamy swirly waves and rudely screeching seagulls. The sun was getting hot.

"I wish there was a place to buy drinks," grumbled Tommy MacCarthy. "I could really use a soda. I can't go the whole day without soda."

"Why didn't you pack one in your lunch, then?" asked Patty.

"I thought you could buy it at the snack bar on board," said Tommy. "Like on the ferries to the islands, you know."

"Here," I said. "You can have some of mine."

Tommy looked in surprise at the can I was holding out to him. "No thanks," he said. Some of the other boys giggled. Tommy started sniggering too. You'd think I had offered to kiss him or something. Those boys act so dumb around girls, I swear. I didn't even particularly like Tommy! I was just trying to be nice!

Corinne was kicking the bench we were sitting on. "Stop kicking, please," I implored. I had this knot in my stomach that kept moving up higher. What if we didn't get to see any whales?

"This is boring," Corinne whined. "I'm hot. Mr. Peake, I don't see any whales. When are we going to see some whales? Are you *sure* we're going to see some? *Promise?*"

"Shut up, Corinne," I hissed.

I felt sorry for Mr. Peake, taking such a bunch of whiners on an adventure they didn't even deserve. No wonder we hadn't seen any whales yet. I was worried he'd get mad and tell the captain to turn back.

But Mr. Peake wasn't paying any attention to Corinne's whining. He was looking through his binoculars. Suddenly he jumped up.

"Thar she blows!" he shouted. We all turned to look. There, in the distance, was a faint fountain of what looked like steam, spouting into the air.

"Is that one?" I squeaked, my voice tight with excitement. "Is that *really* a whale?" I was on my feet, jumping up and down.

Mr. Peake grinned. "It sure is. A beaut!"

My first real live whale! I ran over to the railing, breathless.

Captain Segal yelled, "Hold on tight, everyone. We're on our way!"

He swung the boat around, and we started barreling toward the whale. The waves slapped loudly at the hull, as if the sea was trying to stop us from going that way. Mr. Peake turned to us. "See, kids?" he said. "O ye of little faith!"

Therese, the whale researcher on board, picked up her microphone and started announcing to the rest of the passengers that a whale had been spotted. "Note the double blowhole," she shouted. "See how the spray comes out in two jets? And do you see those knobby bumps all over the head and flippers? Those features tell us it's a humpback whale. In a minute, if it will do us the favor of turning over, you'll get a view of the long white flippers they have. Humpbacks have the longest flippers of any sea mammal. Yep, that's a humpback, all right."

The whole class made a beeline for the deck where you had the best view. I barreled my way through the crowd to the railing and managed to capture a good place at the front. People were pressing against me from the back. "All right, all right, don't *push*!" I yelled, elbowing somebody out of my way with one arm and shielding my eyes against the sun with the other.

As we steamed toward the spouting whale, I could suddenly see three or four more black backs slapping against the foaming waves.

"Ladies and gentlemen, I think we have more than one out there!" called Therese.

"There's another one in back of us," Nick screamed from the stern. "Look, everybody!"

I saw Molly struggling with her camera and suddenly remembered that I had Alex's camera around my neck. I unslung it and took the lens cap off. My fingers were shaking. "More whales over there!" Mr. Peake called from somewhere behind me. "At nine o'clock! What do you think, Therese? Those aren't humpbacks, are they?"

"No sir, those are finbacks," Therese announced over the mike. "They're a mixed bunch, all right!"

"Oh my God!" screeched Corinne. "Look over there! Look, Mr. Peake! More whales!"

It was happening so fast I just didn't know where to look. Everywhere you turned—in front of us, behind us, on either side—you could see whales swooping, surfacing, swimming majestically toward us, whooshing and blowing their spouts loudly, like trumpeters in a giants' marching band.

"This is so—unbelievable!" I gasped.

"Unbelievable," whispered Mr. Peake, but there was an edge of uncertainty in his voice. It gave me a chill.

"Ladies and gentlemen, this is unprecedented," came Therese's voice over the loudspeaker. "I have never witnessed this many whales all in one place!"

Everyone was quiet suddenly. There was a fishy taste to the air. A stinky mist was raining down on us—the steam from dozens and dozens of blowholes. We all stared out at the sea, so calm just a few minutes ago, now a bubbling, snorting mass of great gray, black, and white-bellied bodies rolling gently together.

"What . . . what does it mean?" asked Kristen in a high-pitched voice.

"I have no idea," said Mr. Peake. "Somehow we have stumbled upon a great congregation of whales."

"A congregation of whales!" I whispered dreamily.

"By God, we're surrounded," boomed Captain Segal. He had switched off the engine. "I have never seen this happen. Have you ever heard of this happening, Therese?"

"Never," said Therese. She sounded confused and a little uncertain. There was a silence. Then she went on, her professional announcer's voice coming back. "Ladies and gentlemen, whales don't usually travel in packs. The big whales, for the most part, are loners. And the species don't often mix, although there is evidence that they are able to communicate with each other cross-species. But these . . . look—minke whales, I believe, over there; at three o'clock you can see a whole tribe of finbacks. Those smaller ones jumping over there are pilot whales. I think I saw a couple of grays just a minute ago—I'm sorry, I'm having a hard time identifying them, there are so many! Usually all we see when we go out here off the cape are the humpbacks. They're on their way to their feeding grounds, up north. Wait—over there, behind the others, see it? That big one. Oh my God, it's enormous! Must be at least a ninety-footer, if not more. Can that be a blue whale, Captain?"

"I'm not sure, but you may be right," the captain said slowly. "I've never seen a blue in these parts before. That's a rare sight. Very rare."

They were both quiet for a minute or so.

"Well, get out your cameras, class. Might as well document this. We'll have quite a story to tell when we get home!" said Mr. Peake.

"*If* we ever get home," muttered one of the ship's crew standing behind him, a scruffy sailor in stained gray sweats.

"What shall we do?" said Mr. Peake, turning to Captain Segal, who was giving the sailor an angry stare.

"There's no need to panic, anyway," the captain said. "We'll have to stay put for a while. Until they decide to leave. There's no way out."

"Wouldn't they get out of our way if we restarted the engine?" Jameel suggested.

"I don't know. I wouldn't want to risk alarming this lot," said Captain Segal.

"I want to go home!" wailed Corinne.

"Shhh!" said Jameel. "Let's all stay real quiet. We don't want to make them mad; they might attack the boat."

"Could that happen?" whimpered Kristen, removing her sunglasses and rubbing her eyes. "I mean—do you think they're going to attack the boat?" Molly, who was standing next to me, shuddered and hugged me, giggling with excitement.

"Let's stay calm, everybody," said Mr. Peake. "We'll just observe them quietly, and hopefully they'll get bored and leave us alone."

I couldn't understand the fear and panic in the others' voices. What was there to be afraid of? I only felt elated, and awed, as if I was a witness to some great miracle.

Just below me I saw an eye, a great big eye, looking up at me. It belonged to a humpback—about half the length of our boat. I leaned over the railing for a better look. My whale came in closer.

"Watch it, Iggie!" Molly squealed.

"Don't lean out so far, Isabel," warned Mr. Peake.

"I don't know, Mr. Peake, I think they're trying to communicate with us," I said to him over my shoulder. "I don't think they mean us any harm." I was proud that unlike the others, I wasn't afraid. I stepped up onto the bottom railing, as if to prove my fearlessness, and stretched out my arm. I had this urge to touch the whale's slick knobby head.

What I felt was surprisingly soft, smooth, and cool. It felt so much like human skin, it scared me. I snatched my hand back, my heart pounding. But the whale stayed close to the boat, as if waiting for me to do it again. It was now lying on its side, one of its great white flippers pointing up to the sky, and I saw its big soft round eye again. I could have sworn it was trying to tell me something.

I leaned out again and stretched my arm toward the flipper. Mr. Peake yelled *"Isabel!"* but I ignored him. I stepped up onto the bench, the rail digging into my stomach. Grandly, slowly, the flipper waved at me, and my whale backed off, swimming a few lengths away from the boat. *Oh, don't go, don't go!* I prayed, fumbling with my camera. *At least let me take your picture!* I brought the camera up to my eye. The automatic focus started making its tiny whirring sounds.

Suddenly the whale turned. Half lifting itself out of the water, then coming down with a thundering crash, it blew a great hiss of steam high into the air and came racing back to where I was perched. The kids around me started shrieking; the salty spray rained down on our heads, drenching us. Before I could figure out what was happening, the great creature reared up out of the water like a glistening black torpedo, its side smacking the side of the boat, its huge grinning head towering over me.

I screamed, and the camera slipped out of my grasp. In awesome slow motion, I saw Alexander's prize Minolta sail through the air.

"No!" I cried, lunging for the camera with both arms outstretched. In the same horrible moment, there was a second jolt as another whale rammed the boat from behind.

"Iggie! Isabel!" I heard screaming behind me. *"Hold on!"*

But it was too late. The next thing I knew, I was hurtling through the air. I was falling, down, down, with nothing to hold on to, the wet wind sucking at my hair and the foamy water speeding toward my face. *"Man overboard!"* I heard from somewhere above me.

The cold seawater struck me with such force it took my breath away. I felt the air being pressed out of my body, as if my chest was being wrapped up in giant rubber bands.

The heavy water closed over my head and began pushing me down toward the bottom of the deep. I could feel, rather than see, the light above me getting fainter and the darkness coming closer. I tried to struggle, but the weight of the water pinned my arms to my sides, and I sank like a stone.

three

ALEX is going to kill me.

So what, I'm dead anyway, and he'll be sorry. He'll cry, and wish he'd been nicer to me when he still had the chance.

Why did I have to do it? No one else on board leaned out too far. No one else was a show-off like me. Serves me right.

I'm too young to die. But this is it. I'm drowning, aren't I? And I can't do a thing about it.

Oh my God, this is so bad. The sea is so cold, and so huge, and so deep.

I'm so alone. I can't breathe.

Suddenly I realized that none of it was true.

I wasn't drowning. At least, I didn't think so. I felt as if a giant balloon was being blown into my belly and my chest and my back and it was pushing out the panic, making room for calm. All of a sudden I felt lighter than air. No need to be afraid. The water didn't feel so cold anymore either—it felt pretty comfortable, as a matter of fact, and I could move my arms and legs again. One kick of my legs and I stopped falling. I was now floating horizontally, feeling my heart recover from the jackhammering panic of a moment before.

I wasn't alone, either. I saw bodies, lots of bodies, large, mottled, gray and black and deep blue bodies, above me and below me. The whales! They were everywhere I looked. They looked different down here, below the surface. They seemed longer, slimmer than I'd expected. They moved with the utmost grace, in a slinky slow-motion glide. They were aware of me. They all stared at me with their dark calm eyes. And there were even more of them behind, hovering in the misty distance. Weird as it might seem, I wasn't afraid of them at all. One of them came up and nuzzled me gently. I didn't draw back but let it sort of sniff me all over, front to back, like a dog greeting another dog. It felt nice, like a caress. Another one came over and did the same thing. And another, and another.

And all this time I was feeling very happy, thinking, *This is great, wait till Alex and Jacob hear about this, they never got this close when they went on their whale watch. . . .*

Then it dawned on me that I'd been underwater a pretty long time. Shouldn't my lungs be bursting? I looked up at the green light far above me and decided I'd better go up for air. I kicked my legs, and without too much effort I rose steadily to the surface. Five or six of the whales rose right alongside me, and I couldn't help grinning. I couldn't get over how friendly they were.

My head broke through the surface, which was churning with foam, bubbles spitting and sizzling all around me. The whales that had surfaced with me were merrily snorting steam from their spouts. I was getting drenched, but of course I'd been wet to start with. I felt like laughing out loud.

I saw the *Explorer* rolling in the waves at some distance, and a lifeboat bobbing a few lengths beyond it. Mr. Peake and a crew member were standing in the bow, anxiously scanning the water. "Over here!" I yelled, but at the same time there was a whale sound, like the boom of a foghorn, in my ear. I tried to clear my throat and called again. Again my voice got drowned out. "Hey, you guys," I muttered at the whales, "give me a little room here. And shut the heck up for a minute."

"Isabel."

I turned around. I was sure I'd just heard someone call my name.

But the boats were still far off, too far for them to hear me.

The whales seemed quieter now. They had formed a sort of protective circle around me. No wonder they couldn't see me from the boats.

"Iz-zabel."

I heard it again. A nice, booming sort of voice. Neither male nor female: resonating and low.

"Where?" I called.

"Here."

I turned around again and searched the waters. But all I could see nearby was the foam and the whales.

"Who *are* you?" I gargled. My mouth was full of water.

"Friends," I heard. *"We are your friends. We are the whales."*

"Oh, come off it," I sputtered. I must be going nuts! I was imagining that I could hear the whales talk. Give me a break!

"It is hard for you to understand. We know that."

This was really too ridiculous. I had to stop listening to the voices inside my head and start doing something to attract attention from the boat. They still hadn't spotted me. *I've got to yell real loud,* I thought, *and wave my arms above my head.*

I tried to wave my arms, but it was a very strange feeling, wrong somehow. Before I knew it my body was lifted out of the water, way out, and then I was falling like a stone. I landed with a loud smack. It stung like anything.

"Whoa," I gasped. What was going on! I decided I'd better not make another move.

"Iz-zabel."

"What?" *Leave me alone* is what I meant.

"You are a whale now," came the voice.

"Are you talking to me?" I whispered. I'd had my eyes closed tight since my belly flop. I didn't want to open them.

"Iz-zabel. You. One of us. You are one of the whales."

Oh my God.

"You must not be frightened. You are the Chosen One."

I still refused to open my eyes. But I realized I did feel—different. *Very* different. For one thing, I couldn't seem to spread my legs. When I moved them, they moved in unison, as if they were tied together at the knees. And there was no denying that either the whales had shrunk, or I had grown. A lot. And then there was that light feeling inside my chest and back. And my eyes were playing tricks on me too. Instead of seeing the world in one picture in front of me, it was as if I'd been seeing two different pictures—one on one side, and one on the other.

I opened my eyes. Just to check.

Oh my God. My eyes were still doing it. The two separate pictures. And the whales were still all around me, staring at me.

I twisted my body around to bring my legs into one of the pictures—the picture on the right.

I didn't see any legs. I saw a wide flat tail. Two flukes. A whale's tail!

I started to whimper. I wanted this dream to end now. Now! I wanted to be back in the boat, or better still, back in my own bed, where I was sure I must be lying that very minute, dreaming this horrible dream.

"Don't be sad. Please. It is meant to be."

"How can it be?" I was so confused. Things like this didn't really happen. People don't just turn into whales. What was going on?

The voice seemed to be reading my mind. *"You are not the first. You are one of the Chosen. It is not the first time."*

The voice was coming from the humpback who had first sniffed me, down below the water. He was the closest to me. Or maybe it was a she. How could you tell?

"I am Onijonah, and I am a female. I am your friend."

It freaked me out, the way she read my mind.

"Come now. The others are waiting to greet you."

Wait a minute. *Wait a minute!* How about the boat? Mom, Dad? Mr. Peake? My dumb brothers? My friends?

"*Your people will be sad. They will miss you. You will miss them. But there is nothing you can do about that now.*"

"How can you say that? I've got to tell them! If I don't come home, they'll think I've drowned!"

"*It is unfortunate. But it can't be helped. It is your destiny. You are a whale now.*"

Slow down, slow down. This was all going too fast for me. It was pretty hard to take.

"Prove it," I sputtered. "Prove to me that you are telling the truth and this isn't some weird dream."

She was silent for a minute. Then she said, "*Listen to your heart. Your heart will speak. And your heart will tell you the truth.*"

I closed my eyes and tried to listen to what my heart was telling me.

Oh my God.

I remember being told by Onijonah to take a deep breath—that part was easy—and follow her. That was harder; it took me three tries, because the first two times I tried to dive, my head just bobbed back up to the surface, and it wasn't until I realized I had to fling my legs (excuse me, my tail) high up in the air that I managed it, diving straight down, way back into that murky blackness that had terrified me so only a few minutes before. Now it seemed like a pleasant enough place to be. I tried to close off my mind to all the questions that were zigzagging around in my head like bumper cars, like *What's a Chosen One?* and *Why me?*

When we reached the seabed, the whales installed me on top of a mass of waving seaweed, soft and tickly as feathers, with Onijonah at my side. The other whales then formed themselves into a sort of huge reception line that stretched for miles and snaked around and around us in the most orderly way.

And then came my introduction to the whales. For what seemed like hours I was inspected and nuzzled by hundreds of whales. Once in a while we'd swim back up to the surface for some deep breaths, and then we'd dive down again to continue the ceremony. I had never thought I'd get to see so many of them up close. Sperm whales and orcas. Minkes and finbacks. Pygmy pilot whales and snow-white belugas. Grinning fat bow-headed whales and gigantic blue whales. I'd studied them all in books, but here they were so real, so magnificent, so majestic! They looked so different, in fact, from the way they were drawn in the pictures and posters I used to collect that I realized no illustration could do them justice.

It seemed they all wanted to meet me. They were in very good spirits, considering how long some of them had to wait in line. Some were shy and passed by me very quickly, just glancing at me out of one eye, then hurrying on. Others swam around me, above me and below me, or looked me straight in the eye. One or two hummed a little tune for me, and others made me laugh with their jumps and flips and jagged moves. Onijonah stayed by my side the whole time and told me their names together with the sort of things they liked to do, like: "Bonahdiboh, lord of the ice floe," or "Fanbelly, swims with tuna."

"What did you say his name was again?" I whispered to Onijonah.

"Who?" she asked.

"That humpback who said he was your cousin," I said.

"Humpback?" Onijonah exclaimed. Then she laughed. "Humpback!"

"What's so funny?" I said.

"Is that what you call us?" She laughed some more.

I realized that maybe I had hurt her feelings.

"I'm sorry," I said. "That's what—I mean, in books, my teacher, the researcher on the ship—everybody calls whales that look like you. Is that wrong?"

The old minke whale to whom I had just been introduced winked at me. "They are a little touchy, her tribe," he whispered. "Some say that humans used to call them not only that, but worse things too, like 'knucklehead.'"

"Who are you calling a knucklehead!" boomed a heavyset humpback behind him, giving him a nip on the flukes.

"We are called the Singing Ones," Onijonah explained to me with great dignity. "Otherwise known as the Sirens. We are a very ancient and proud tribe."

"And so you *should* be," said the old minke hastily, fanning his tail from side to side.

"But I didn't mean . . . ," I stammered.

"No offense. There is so much for you to learn," she sighed, and gave me a comforting pat on the back with her flipper. "Where were we? Oh yes, my cousin. His name is Jessaloup."

"Jessaloup," I repeated. It suited him. He was a handsome

whale, a deep black, with a strong jaw, a smattering of hair-knobs, and bright white-and-black-patterned flukes. He had looked at me with a smirk, a cheeky "I've got your number" look. I was glad he was Onijonah's cousin. I had the feeling I would be seeing more of him.

It turned out I was a Siren too. (Of course Jessaloup, who later heard of my blunder, insisted on calling me the Hump. To tell you the truth, the way he had with nicknames reminded me a lot of my brothers.) The idea took some getting used to. I mean, Sirens have a flat knobby lid for a head, a tanklike lower jaw and throat, and eyes stuck halfway down the body, just in front of those goofy-looking white flippers. It would be a while before I could appreciate the beauty of this body that was now mine. The only thing I liked about it then was the elegance of my curvy tail.

I wasn't a full-sized Siren, I was only about three-quarters grown. That made me a pretty small whale, by their standards.

"Onijonah!" I whispered during the next breathing break, my heart pounding because it had just occurred to me. "Onijonah, how big am I, exactly?"

She chuckled. "I would say you are about four flippers."

"I mean, in human length!"

"Human length? Hmm. I would say you are about five of your tallest men's lengths, end to end."

I couldn't help grinning. I was about as tall as five pro basketball stars. As tall as the Chicago Bulls, or the New York Knicks, standing on each other's shoulders! "Wow!" I breathed. "I must weigh a ton!"

"Probably," she said nonchalantly. "Tons, actually. But

only on land. In the ocean, it does not matter how much you weigh. Since we float, we are weightless."

"W-wow!" I said again. I was having a hard time getting a handle on how big I was. As big as a school bus! As big as our garage! Much bigger than an elephant, bigger than two elephants, as big as three or four elephants, maybe! I felt dizzy at the thought. And yet I didn't *feel* that huge. I felt pretty light and nimble, to tell you the truth.

Then I got the giggles. I started shaking helplessly, unleashing streams of bubbles from my blowhole. I was thinking of my aunt Madeline, who has this totally annoying habit of taking one look at my brothers and me, opening her eyes wide, putting both her hands to her mouth, and exclaiming to my mother, "My, how they have *grown*, Mona!"

If only Aunt Madeline could see me now!

Onijonah said they were all amazed by my smooth skin. Most of them had barnacles and even seaweed growing all over their tails and heads and fins, and I could see that many of the big ones had nasty-looking white and brown scars all over. "You look like a newborn calf!" one nice old female boomed as she inspected me. "So smooth!"

"Wait till you've been in this soup a few weeks," mouthed a sassy young thing behind her. "You'll get encrusted soon enough. I can show you some good rocks to scrape off the worst of it, if you like."

"Thank you," I giggled. "That's good to know." *I guess!* I thought. *What do I know!*

In the end I got a little light-headed, laughing too much, and turning around too quickly so that I kept bumping into other whales and slapping them with my tail, and whales don't like getting bumped into like that. So Onijonah decided I should take a little nap, and that the whales should leave me alone until I got more used to the idea of being a whale. She took me up to the surface and explained that I would have to sleep floating near the top, so that my airhole was exposed to the air; otherwise I'd drown. I laughed at that, too; the idea of a whale drowning was sort of amusing to me right then. But she didn't think it was so funny, and when I opened one eye and found her floating right beside me, her watchful eye on me, I realized that she was going to make sure I didn't sink.

I yawned and got a mouthful of salty water. "Thanks, Onijonah," I gurgled sleepily.

"No problem," she said.

I slept.

four

WHEN I woke up it was just getting dark. The last glimmers of light were skittering across the rippling water, like a little tune dancing over the keys of one of those old player pianos.

I had sort of expected to find myself back home, or at least back on board the *Explorer*. But with a sinking feeling I realized, from the way I was lying in the water next to Onijonah, that I was still a whale.

This was getting serious.

"Onijonah!" was the first thing I said. "Tell me the truth. Am I dead? Is that why I'm here?"

"Dead?" she said. "Oh no, not at all. You are not dead."

"Whew!" I said. I thought it over a moment. "So . . . if

I'm not dead, then there's no reason—I mean, when can I go home?"

"You can't go home," she said. "At least, not for the time being."

"Why?" I said. "You *said* I wasn't dead!" I was thinking of my family, probably sitting down to dinner without me by now, wondering why I hadn't come home. If I wasn't home by bedtime, I'd be in *big* trouble. Then I started trembling—did they think I had drowned? They must be out of their minds with worry!

"You can't go home because you're not a human anymore," said Onijonah.

I suppressed a sob. "I know that," I said. "I realize I've turned into a whale. But I *want* to go home!"

"You will—someday." Her voice was very gentle. "But not yet."

"But—*why?*"

The thing about whales is, you don't have to spell stuff out for them the way you have to do with humans. I think that's because their language is much more layered than our language. Every sound can mean zillions of different things. If that seems complicated, it really isn't. Not if you are a whale yourself.

Onijonah seemed to know exactly what I meant.

"Why have *you* been Chosen?" said Onijonah. "Child, that is for us to find out. There is always a reason. A good reason. I can only tell you we knew you were coming and have been waiting for you a long time—"

"How long?" I interrupted.

"Oh, around eleven or twelve years," she said.

"That's about when I was born," I said.

"Exactly," she said, as if that settled it.

I was more confused than ever. "But *how* did you know? Who told you?"

"All the whales know. It is like a message."

"But who gives you the message?"

She thought about that for a moment, then said carefully, "Each whale is the messenger. Every one of us. It is in the air we breathe. It's in the water. It's in the Song."

I said a minute ago that whales can explain everything in one sentence. But that doesn't mean I could understand it. My head was spinning.

Onijonah seemed to read my mind again. "That is why so many of our brethren journeyed to our ocean today. We all knew you were coming. It was in the Song."

"Okay, but . . . ," I began.

"Yes?" said Onijonah.

"If you knew I was coming today, if it was in this Song you're talking about, shouldn't you also know when I get to go home?"

"Oh, child," she said. "We'll just have to see about that, won't we."

"But . . ." I was ready to start bawling like a baby. *Mom! I was thinking. Daddy! Molly and Kristen! Alex and Jacob! I'll never see them again! I'll never be able to tell them what happened! It's the coolest thing that's ever happened to me, or anybody I know, and now they'll never find out about it!*

"Don't be sad," Onijonah said gently. "The Song tells us the Chosen One will stay long enough to learn, and to fulfill her task. Then she may go home."

"But how long—" I started again.

"Come," said Onijonah firmly, "it is time for the Ceremony."

There was a loud bang behind me, like a gunshot. Then another one. Startled, I looked around. In the distance, some young whales were cavorting in the waves. The sound I was hearing was the report of their flippers slapping the surface. "What ceremony?" I asked, turning back to Onijonah. "I thought we'd finished the ceremony."

"We finished the Introductions," explained Onijonah. "Now we begin the Ceremony."

"Can't I just do what *they're* doing instead?" I complained. I could see where the expression "having a whale of a time" came from. There was a lot of splashing, twisting, rolling, and diving going on out there. So far, being a whale had been a pretty serious business. If I had to be one of them, I might as well start having some fun with it, I figured.

"There will be plenty of time for play later," Onijonah said. "We cannot keep the others waiting. Some of them have far to travel tonight. Besides, the Ceremony will address more of your questions."

"How do you know I want to ask any more questions?" I sulked.

"Come," she said. With a flick of her tail, she was gone.

I sighed. Then, panicked at the thought of being left alone up there, I took a deep breath the way I'd been shown, and dove.

Later, I wished I'd been able to pay more attention during the Ceremony. But I was in such a giddy mood that night that a lot of it didn't sink in—not in the right way.

They told me to lie with my head down, at a forty-five-degree angle, my tail just touching the surface. Facing me was an enormous blue whale, at least three times my size, floating in the same position, her head down and her tail just below the surface. I recognized her as one of the first whales I'd been introduced to, and I remembered her name: Indigoneah, Keeper of Songs. Onijonah had whispered to me that of all the visiting whales, I should show her the most respect, because she was the largest and also the wisest of the whales in our ocean. Onijonah was floating at right angles to us, forming the third spoke of the wheel. Facing her was a very old bull-nosed sperm whale, General Trogulo. Onijonah told me he was the leader of the toothed whales, "the warriors of the sea," she called them. The other whales positioned themselves in two circles around and slightly below us—a tight inner circle, and a much wider outer circle. The inner circle seemed to be composed of the largest whales. I later found out that they were the elders. They held themselves very still, hanging head down, like us. From the corner of my eye I could see the smaller whales in the looser outer circle, a less disciplined bunch, fidgeting and jostling each other.

I was instructed to take as deep a breath as possible at the surface before taking my place. I took three or four breaths of fresh sea air, to calm myself. Then, pushing in with my flippers, I slowly sank under the water.

"Commence the Ceremony!" boomed the blue whale.

"Commence the Ceremony!" echoed the other whales. There was a pause while they all looked at me expectantly. "Uh, commence the Ceremony," I quavered.

All eyes swiveled back to Indigoneah, and I coughed with relief.

"Merchild," said Indigoneah. "Be one of us."

"Be one of us!" the others chanted.

"Be with us," the blue whale continued.

"Be with us!" they chorused.

I looked anxiously over at Onijonah. I didn't know what was expected of me. She shook her head, as if I shouldn't worry so much.

"Isabel," the old whale sang.

"Isabel!" the congregation repeated after her.

"Hear our Song," said the blue whale, softly.

"Hear our Song!" they all sang out.

"O merchild, O Chosen One, hear our Song," sang the blue whale, "and be one with us."

"Be one with us!" came the chorus.

There was a commotion: a group of about two dozen whales pushed their way into the inner circle. They were all Sirens. Jessaloup was one of them. With their white bellies, long white flippers, and black backs, they looked like an orchestra in tuxedos. They arranged themselves head down in a half circle. There was a hush. The choir looked over at Indigoneah, who nodded. They stiffened, and without moving their mouths, they began the Song.

It was the strangest sound I have ever heard: mellow and rasping, melodious and harsh, high and low, rapid and slow, snickering and smooth, shockingly loud and achingly soft. I couldn't make out any words.

The Song went on for a long time. What I understood, at first, was very little, but what I *felt* was indescribable. The sound tugged at my heart and sent shivers down my spine and along my flukes. I felt a lump in my throat, and my blubber vibrated with every note.

What the Song seemed to be about was the history of the land, and the history of the ocean, and how the whales fit into it, and how they were related to every other living thing on earth. At least, I think that's what it was about, because that was the picture that came into my head as I listened: a picture of a world teeming with living things, each in its proper place, plus the tides, and the stars, and the moon, and the sun, and the rocks, and the reefs, and the clouds, all swirling in a slow, lovely dance. I stared into space, enjoying the dazzling pictures in my head.

Then the tune changed and the notes became shorter and weirder, but strangely familiar. Startled, I looked up. The whales were gazing at me mournfully. The Song was coming in gasps and loud upbursts now, with interludes of trilling notes. Then I understood what they were singing about now: they were singing about me, about us, about mankind! And there was a sadness that had not been there before. The Song was now one long question. Suddenly I was afraid of what I might hear. I didn't want to listen anymore. I looked away and tried thinking about something else.

Abruptly, the Song ended, and the singers swam back into the ranks.

There was a long silence.

"Isabel," came Onijonah's voice, very gentle. "Perhaps it would help if we answered some of your questions now." I could hardly look at her. I felt I had let her down.

I didn't say anything.

"We are your friends," prodded Indigoneah. "No need to be afraid."

I was waiting for the chorus to echo her words, as before. But they didn't, and that made me feel just a little better. To be honest, it felt terrible right then, being the center of all the attention like that. Before, while the Introductions had been going on, I had felt flattered, important. Now I wished they would all just look the other way. I could have paid more attention to the Song if only they hadn't all been staring at me, like something was expected of me. I wished I could be invisible, I wished I could have been watching all this on TV, so they couldn't see me.

"Okay," I said. It was strange hearing my own voice. It sounded very thin and faint. I guess the echo of the Song was still ringing in my ears. "Sure, I have questions. Who wouldn't!"

Indigoneah smiled. She probably thought I was being a wise guy. "Go on," she said.

"I mean, I go on an ordinary field trip with my class, only I fall overboard, but instead of drowning I turn into a whale. It doesn't make much sense, you know."

I just saw all these eyes, rows and rows of eyes, looking at me expectantly.

"Excuse me a moment," I said, and swung up to the surface. The sea was an immense gray blanket gently swaying.

There was not a boat in sight. The seagulls had disappeared into the night. The stars were just pinpricks in the stark black sky, shivering in the cold. Not a living thing anywhere, not a spout, not a bubble on the surface to hint at the gigantic hoedown just below me. I considered running away, just heading out and leaving them all behind. But that was ridiculous—where would I go, looking like a whale? Home? Not a chance!

I took a couple of deep, loud, sputtering breaths. Then I dove under again. They were all still there, exactly as before, watching me.

I decided not to be a wise guy anymore. If they could be serious, I could be serious.

"What does it mean, 'chosen'?" I asked.

"Not every human being becomes a whale," she said. "You have to be chosen."

"Who does the choosing, then?"

"The world, of course," she said.

I sighed. "You said I wasn't the only one," I went on, trying a new approach. I really wanted to understand. "Who were the others?"

"Oh, there have been so many! At one time, when humans were new on the land, many, *many* were chosen."

"Yeah, like who?" I challenged.

"Like—Jonah," she said. "For instance."

"Jonah?" I repeated, suspiciously.

"Most humans know of Jonah," said Indigoneah. "But perhaps you are too young."

"Of course I know the story!" I sputtered. "You mean the guy in the Bible who was trying to run away from God, and there was a big storm, and his shipmates threw him overboard?"

Indigoneah nodded, and so did Onijonah and General Trogulo.

"But you've got it wrong!" I said. "Jonah was *swallowed* by a whale!"

"That is what you humans made of the story. What really happened was that Jonah was a human who was chosen to live as a whale. He returned to his own kind with much wisdom to teach. Someday, when you are ready for it, you will hear his song."

So you all think I failed the test, I thought. *Well, I don't care. I don't need to understand your stupid songs.*

Onijonah threw me a reproachful glance.

"But anyway, that was in the old days," I said quickly. "That was way back, before modern times—before . . . when there were miracles and things, I mean. It doesn't happen now."

"It is true that in recent times there have been fewer and fewer Chosen Ones," Indigoneah said mournfully. "That is why there has been so much interest in your arrival. The last mermaid—"

"Mermaid? Wait a minute!" I interrupted.

Indigoneah paused.

"Mermaid? Please! No, come off it. Are we talking about *mermaids* now?" I scoffed. "What's that got to do with anything? Mermaids only exist in fairy tales!"

"Of course. I am sorry. I am confusing you. No. Mermaid is what we whales call your kind. Sea-maid. Sea, or *Mer,* in one of your languages. Mer-man, mer-maid, mer-person. Didn't you know that? Maid of the Sea."

"Oh!" I said. I felt a little dazed. "I see!" I twisted my head around so that I could just catch a glimpse of my elegant flukes. The lower half of my body looked just like a mermaid's tail. "Oh my God," I said. "You mean, *I* am . . . a mermaid?"

"Of course you are a mermaid, Chosen One. Or merperson, if you prefer."

I shook my flukes in wonder. I, Isabel, a mermaid! What next! Jonah was a whale and sirens and mermaids really existed, only they weren't what we'd always imagined, they were actually whales!

Indigoneah continued calmly, "Our last mermaid was an Inuk, from up north. Her name was ApigonNga. She had always loved whales and asked her spirits to let her join us. It was a fruitful exchange. She brought about a new understanding between us and her people."

"There was, before, Mortimer, and Mermanmelvil, and Carmelina, and Kukua," intoned General Trogulo.

"Herculyssus and Aegea, Rebacabeca and Penocyo, Vishnu and Suyura," Onijonah finished. "And many, many more."

"But how come I never heard of them, then?"

"Because there are many songs, merchild, that you do not know."

"No?"

"No."

I didn't exactly buy it. If I had never heard of them,

maybe they had vanished from the human world for good. Like all those people who kept disappearing into the Bermuda Triangle. They were never heard from again either.

Was that what was going to happen to me?

In closing, Indigoneah went on to announce to the whales, in a solemn voice, that Onijonah had been chosen to be my guardian and my teacher. And then she said something else.

"Isabel," she said. "You understand that your mission now is to learn as much as you can of our ways."

"Sure," I said. "I guess." I wasn't too happy about it. The way she said it, it sounded pretty final. A mission: it sounded like they were expecting me to be around for a long time. To tell you the truth, I was already feeling really homesick, and she kept making it worse.

"But another task awaits you as well."

"It does?" I said.

"And that is, you must help *us* to understand."

"Help us understand!" the other whales droned.

"Teach us," said Indigoneah.

"Teach us," sang the congregation.

"Okay," I said. "I mean, I'll try." I was beginning to feel a little better, because I realized the whales hadn't really expected me to understand the Song. And now they were all being really nice, because they realized I was scared, and homesick, and they wanted me to feel good about myself again.

Then they did something to make me feel even better.

Indigoneah opened and closed her mouth three times and belched out a great balloon of bubbles that drifted up to the surface. At that signal, the other whales of the inner circle began swimming around me, slowly at first, then faster and faster, each whale pushing streams of bubbles out of its mouth and blowhole. Soon I was surrounded by a dense wall of bubbles, a whirling tornado of white bubbles that caught me like a fish in a net, swirling around me and underneath me, and then lifting me up and pushing me steadily toward the surface. I burst through into the cool night air in an explosion of fizzing, boiling water.

"W-wow!" I exclaimed. The swirling water was swooshing me around and around, like the last few inches of water emptying out of a bathtub. It was great. I felt dizzy and elated and special.

I also understood that this was the finale, the sign that the Ceremony was over, and a way for the whales to say goodbye to me.

"Bye, Isabel, good luck!" I heard as the whales started to swim away from me in all directions.

"Goodbye!" I sputtered, still spinning around, but more slowly now. I waved a flipper at them.

"Goodbye, merchild," boomed Indigoneah in my ear. I turned toward her, only to see her heavy tail lifting starkly out of the water as she sounded and disappeared from view.

I looked around. Only about a dozen whales—all Sirens—remained behind, including Onijonah and Jessaloup. They were swimming around, stretching their backs and their flukes, and chatting with each other, like a family relaxing after the party guests have gone.

"All right," said Onijonah, rapping her flipper on the water, all business once more. "We have had the Introductions and the Ceremony. Now we begin the Training."

five

My training as a whale started that very night. Night and day don't mean very much if you are a whale, since a whale's days are not divided up into mealtimes and bedtimes, the way ours are. If you are a whale, you eat when there is food and nap when you are tired. Darkness doesn't bother whales; they rely more on their ears than on their eyes anyway. That's just as well, because if you swim deep down in the ocean, there isn't enough light to see by, even if it is sunny up above.

"First," said Onijonah, "you must learn to dive properly."

I thought I hadn't been doing a bad job, for a beginner. Did they set me straight! Onijonah and some of her relatives showed me where I had been going wrong. I had been trying to head straight down, slapping my tail down hard on top of the water as I dove.

"That is no good, you see, merchild," said Momboduno, one of the elders. "You slap your tail and it slows your descent."

"But I've seen you slapping your tails on the water," I protested.

"We do that for fun sometimes; or when we want to send a message. You'll learn about that later. But in plain diving, the important thing to remember is to arch your back, lift your tail out as far as you can, and then let it *g-l-i-d-e* in, like so. . . ." As he explained it, he demonstrated the dive, and I saw that as he dove, his tail went in clean as a butter knife, with awesome control. Only the slightest ripples showed where he had gone down.

"Okay, let me try that," I said eagerly, and did it again.

When I came up, I looked at my trainers. "Was that better?"

"There was still a splash," said Momboduno.

"It was better, but you need to lift the flukes up higher," said Onijonah.

I noticed that Jessaloup and some of the younger whales were playing and diving a little farther off. They didn't appear to be very interested in my training. Suddenly Jessaloup breached, doing a beautiful three-quarter spin in the air before coming down with a huge crash. Then he did it again, and a third time. *Show-off,* I thought.

"Can I try that too?" I asked Momboduno and Onijonah.

They laughed. "One step at a time, merchild," said Momboduno. "You work on your diving first. And then we will give you some lessons in swimming. And you have to learn to feed. And to master the three *ing*s, of course."

"The three *ing*s?" I asked. "What are they?"

"The three *ing*s. The most important skills for a Siren's survival: *ring*ing, *ping*ing, and *sing*ing. To hear, to see, and to know. Once you are proficient in those, there *may* be time to try out some acrobatics. Do you agree, Onijonah?"

"Well, yes, perhaps," she said gravely. I knew they were teasing me.

"Oh, all right," I said. To tell you the truth, I was a little disappointed that Jessaloup had not shown any interest in my training.

I practiced my diving—with only one short break for a nap—until the sun came up. Then Onijonah said, "The prey is rising. We can eat."

"I'm hungry!" I said, surprised. *Well, of course I'm hungry*, I told myself: I had had nothing to eat since nibbling at my granola bar on the boat. Only, it wasn't the normal faint nagging sensation I knew as hunger. It was a huge raging commotion in my belly, a kind of ravenous itching in my throat. You know how people sometimes say "I'm so hungry I could eat a horse"—well, I was so hungry right then I could have swallowed a *house*.

"Come," said Onijonah. "Follow me!"

I had a hard time keeping up with the other whales. I didn't slice smoothly through the water like they did, but jerked and shuddered against the buffeting waves like a broken fan belt. I swam as hard as I could, though, splashing awkwardly, pushed on by the gnawing in my belly.

"Where are we going?" I panted. "Can't we just eat right here?"

Onijonah slowed down so I could catch up. "I am sorry. I should have explained. We have received a message from a pod of other Sirens—Hobagil's family—that they have found a rich feeding ground a few thousand lengths from here. That is where we are headed."

"Message? When did you get a message?" I asked. I hadn't noticed anybody approaching us with any message.

"You have much to learn, child," said Onijonah. "The message is the Song. Hobagil has signaled to us from the feeding grounds, in song."

"I guess I wasn't really listening," I said.

"Listening will be the most difficult task for you to master," said Onijonah. "It will take much practice, and much patience."

"I know," I said. The Ceremony had already taught me that.

By the time Onijonah and I got to the feeding ground, the other whales in our party had already joined Hobagil's tribe at their meal. Gangs of screaming seabirds were torpedo-diving into the foaming waves, pecking at the food that had been driven to the surface. The whales paid no attention to them, though. One by one they broke sideways through the surface with their huge mouths wide open, water spilling from their jaws in buckets. Except for a couple of lone stragglers off by themselves, they were drawn up in three or four lines, executing their moves with perfect timing. They looked like an army of steam shovels and backhoes plowing up the sea.

"Dig in, it's delicious and there's plenty!" came a cheerful voice right behind me. I turned and saw Jessaloup with seaweed trailing from his open mouth.

"I don't know how," I said.

"It's easy. First you dive. You know how to do that, don't you?" The way he said it, it sounded a little superior.

"Sure," I said coolly. *No thanks to you,* I thought.

"Okay. You try to dive as smoothly as possible, without a splash, so you don't disturb the food. Then you rise back up, with your mouth wide open, as wide as you can, so you trap it in your mouth."

"Okay," I said eagerly, and made ready to dive.

"Not so fast, I haven't told you the important part yet!" Jessaloup warned.

"You can tell me later!" I gulped as I went down.

A few seconds later I rose to the surface, as Jessaloup had told me to, with my mouth wide open. I felt little fish and shrimpy things squirming around in my throat deliciously. But as I broke through the surface, all of it—the water, the fish, and the krill—came spilling out again in one big gush. I was left with nothing.

"If you had just let me finish, I'd have told you what to do next!" Jessaloup was laughing at me. I guess I must have looked pretty desperate. "As I was saying, when you come up, you've got to push your tongue against your plates so you squeeze out the water and trap the food inside your throat," he said. Then he dove, to demonstrate.

I experimented with pushing my tongue forward against the fringes of soft bone hanging down from the roof of my mouth. I saw what he meant.

To make up for lost time, I dove at once, not waiting for Jessaloup, and this time the food stayed in my mouth, crushed between my tongue and my baleen plates. I finally had the delicious sensation of great gobs of slippery, slimy, crunchy grub sliding down my gullet as I gulped.

For the next few hours I paid no attention to Jessaloup or Onijonah or any of the others but fed myself silly, diving and surfacing, diving and surfacing, enjoying the rhythm, harvesting my little plot of ocean, happy to scratch at the itchy hunger in my throat.

six

My life fell into a pattern of eating, sleeping, training, and swimming. As I got more familiar with the routines of being a whale, I noticed that the water was getting colder. I asked Momboduno about this one day, because it was summer, after all, and by my guess the water should have been getting warmer.

"Ah, yes, but we are on our way north, merchild. That is why it's getting a little cooler. We're heading for the Arctic."

The Arctic? That was the North Pole! A shudder went up my spine. I was getting very far away from home.

"Why?" I asked in a shaky voice. "Why couldn't we just have stayed near the cape—I mean, isn't that very far?"

"We go where the food is plentiful," he explained. "The farther north we go, the more plentiful the harvest. That is why we go there."

I tried not to think of my family back home. I reminded myself sternly that Onijonah's family was now my family. Wherever they chose to go, I'd have to go too. The alternative—being left alone in this enormous, empty sea—wasn't an option for me.

There were twelve whales in our pod, or tribe, including two calves. Tengapoul, Onijonah's mother, was the oldest. No one knew how old she was exactly, but she was said to have given birth to twenty-five children. Most of them were now grown up and having calves of their own. Tengapoul went her own way mostly, feeding a good distance away from the rest of the group, but the family was always in touch with her, signaling to her and checking to see if she needed anything.

The way the whales communicated with each other was sort of like calling each other on the telephone. Underwater, you sent out these sound signals, and when your call reached its destination—another whale several miles away, for instance—it would bounce off that whale and come boomeranging back to where you were. You could tell how far away the other whale was by the time it took for your own sound to come back to you. I remembered reading about this in Mr. Peake's class—it was called echolocation in our textbooks. But the whales just called it ringing.

The way Onijonah and Momboduno taught me to ring was by first having me follow them around and try to recognize their sounds traveling back to them. But soon I learned to make the ringing sounds myself. Ringing was different from talking or singing. You had to make the sound travel out of the top of your head, instead of from deep inside. Then, after I'd mastered ringing, they taught me pinging. At first I had a hard time understanding the difference, but soon I learned that in pinging, instead of letting the sound scatter over a wider area (as you would to find another whale), you focused the vibrations coming out of your head in a single direction. From the ping coming back to you, you could tell if there were any big rocks, or a boat, or a beach, or even a school of fish, right in front of you. Soon I learned to find my way in pitch blackness, just by listening to the sounds I made. It was good to know that if I ever strayed too far from my family, I could always find my way back to them by ringing and pinging. It made the ocean seem a lot smaller somehow, less immense and threatening. More like home.

Apart from Jessaloup, there were four other young male cousins in our group—Bickseye, Lemmertail, Gilrut, and Trog. They hung around together mostly and were forever fooling around and showing off to each other. I loved to watch them leaping and spinning and performing their stunts. They were faster than the rest of us and also seemed much more carefree.

The rest of the pod was made up of the elders and the females. The elders were Onijonah, Momboduno, and Tengapoul; the females were yours truly, Blossamer, who was only a little bigger than me, and two nursing mothers—Dilgruel and Feeonah. Their calves' names were Tomturan and Delight. Sometimes Onijonah made me take lessons with the babies, and even though I loved playing with them—

they were very cute—it could be a little embarrassing. There were times when I felt like a fifth grader who'd been sent back to kindergarten.

Of course it was only at those times that Jessaloup ever took it into his head to notice me.

"So! How's the Hump?" he asked with a smirk, splashing me with his tail while I was treading water, desperately trying to hold my head straight up above the waves. I was supposed to be practicing spy-hopping with Tomturan and Delight.

I choked on a few gallons of seawater. Before I could reply, he'd turned in a graceful swoop and raced off to where his friends were waiting for him.

"I hate you, Jessaloup," I muttered.

"What was that?" asked Onijonah, who had just come up next to me.

"Oh, nothing," I muttered. "Onijonah, can I stop now? I think I know how to do this."

"Look at Tomturan," said Onijonah. "See how steadily he keeps just his eyes above the level of the water, his flippers submerged? That's how I want to see you do it, not all that wild bobbing up and down. You cannot have a complete field of vision above water if you move around like that. Good work, Tomturan, little fellow. Keep practicing, Isabel."

I snorted loudly from my blowhole. It sounded sort of like a raspberry.

The water kept getting colder. It was now almost the end of summer, and we were still heading north. Luckily, with all the eating I had been doing, I had a nice thick coat of blubber to protect me, and I didn't mind the cold too much. It was like playing in the snow when you're dressed warmly from head to toe. On really cold nights we'd all take naps huddled together, side by side. My favorite spot was sandwiched between Onijonah and Delight, the little girl-calf who had adopted me as her big sister.

Playing with Delight and Tomturan wasn't so bad; to tell the truth, I secretly enjoyed it. Sometimes they would take turns latching on to my back with their little flippers and letting me take them for a piggyback ride. Or we'd play a whale version of leapfrog, flipping over and under each other—the object of the game was to try not to be the piggy-in-the-middle. When we got tired, we might swim over to Tengapoul and huddle close to her wrinkly, crusty bulk as she told us a story of the old days, back when she was young. But our favorite game was one that Momboduno had taught us as a way of practicing our ringing and pinging. It was just like hide-and-seek: one of us counted to a hundred while the others swam off and hid. Not only did you have to find the others by ringing and pinging; you also had to learn to recognize the particular ring of your playmates and not confuse them with some other whale or fish swimming in the water. Once, Tomturan thought he'd found Delight and me, and swam right up to a couple of nasty-looking sharks! We didn't realize what had happened until we found him cowering underneath his mother, shaking like a jellyfish. He wouldn't leave her side the rest of the day.

Another time, I was It. It was pretty dusky underwater, so I couldn't see a thing. I started ringing, and soon enough I could hear my ring echoing off two little obstacles, side by side. I knew it was the calves because of the way they were fidgeting and giggling. I decided to sneak up on them from below, to give them a fright. I stopped making any sound, and dove way down. Then I turned and started creeping stealthily up toward them. When I figured I was just two or three lengths below them, I suddenly pumped my tail as hard as I could and shot up at them like a racehorse out of the starting gate.

Ba-bonng!

I'd bumped into something swimming right in my path.

"*Ouch!* Hey! Can't you look where you're going?" It was Jessaloup's voice. "What's the matter with you? Don't you know how to ring?"

I heard Delight and Tomturan laughing their heads off just above us.

"I'm sorry," I muttered. "We were playing a game . . . I didn't realize you were there."

Jessaloup was rubbing his chin, where I'd walloped him with the top of my head. "I should have guessed it was you, Hump."

"I *said* I was sorry!"

"All right, all right!" he said. "Serves me right for coming over to ask if I could play too."

"*You* want to play with *us*?" I said suspiciously.

"Jessaloup! Jessaloup!" The two babies were jiggling up and down excitedly. "Jessaloup, play with us!"

"I will, if *she*'ll let me," he said.

"Sure!" I said brightly. "Why not? I mean, it's a free country."

"Free country?" he repeated, puzzled.

"A free ocean—oh, never mind," I said. "But this time, you're It. Isn't he, kids?"

"Jessaloup is It!" squeaked Delight.

"Hide!" squealed Tomturan.

"Count to a hundred," I instructed. "You do know how to count to a hundred, don't you?" I added sarcastically.

Jessaloup gave me a look.

"And real slow. I mean *s–l–o–w*!"

"Any more instructions?" he drawled.

"We'll try not to make it too hard for you," I said. "Since you're a beginner."

"You'd better get out of here," he growled. "Oo-o-one, two-o-oo . . ."

We took some deep breaths at the surface and then dove straight down, as deep as we could go. We tried not to ping so we wouldn't give ourselves away. The sandy seabed was covered with seaweed as thick and green as cactuses.

"Look!" whispered Tomturan. "Hiding place!"

A large gray shape loomed out of the seaweed forest—a huge dead-looking hulk resting on the bottom of the sea.

"Whale?" asked Delight.

It certainly looked like a very large whale, a Siren, by the knobby look of it. Only it didn't move. And it didn't gleam. It was covered with a fine layer of sand. It looked pretty dead to me. *Don't panic, Isabel,* I thought. *Set a good example.*

Cautiously, we moved in closer.

"Eyes!" said Tomturan, pointing. I shrank back.

And then I saw. Not eyes. Portholes. And the knobs were rivet heads. "A submarine!" I gasped.

I swam over to one of the portholes and glanced in. It was filled to the top with murky water.

"Come!" I whispered. "Let's hide behind it, on the other side. He'll never find us, because all he'll hear is the metal ping."

Exploding with excitement and glee, the two little ones followed me around the back of the sunken hulk.

"Got ya!"

We all three screamed and sprang back.

It was Jessaloup, with his lopsided grin. "Scared you, didn't I!"

I couldn't find my voice; my heart was pounding too hard.

"Uh," I finally said. "No fair! How'd you get here so fast?"

"I am fast," he said simply. "And I heard you gasp a minute or two ago. You gave yourselves away. I didn't cheat, if that's what you think. I counted to a hundred."

I had to admit it was possible, if he'd swum like a streak of lightning. Which I supposed he was capable of doing.

"What have you got here, anyway?" he said. "A dead whale?"

"Submeaney," Delight told him solemnly.

"A what?" said Jessaloup.

"A submarine," I said. My voice had come back. "It's a kind of underwater human ship. It must have sunk years ago. It's all overgrown with seaweed inside."

"Submarine?" he repeated. He seemed impressed. "Are you sure? I've never seen one before."

"Of course I'm sure," I said. "I visited a navy museum once, and they had them there. This is a real old-fashioned one. Probably pretty old. Maybe even a hundred seasons old."

"*Squidfight!*" Jessaloup said. (*Squidfight* means "cool" in whale talk.) I'd finally done something to earn his respect. "A shipwreck! Let's explore!"

I hung back a bit. Tomturan and Delight were hovering behind my flippers.

"Come on!" Jessaloup said. "It's not going to bite you!"

"You first," I muttered.

"Afraid?" he goaded.

"No, but . . ."

Jessaloup swam around the sub, then came back to where I was hovering. "It's all closed up," he said, disappointed. "Do you think we could smash it open?"

"No way," I said. "Those things are made of aluminum and steel. You'd need dynamite to get it open."

Jessaloup had his eye pressed to one of the portholes. "Look at this!" he exclaimed. He waved his flipper at me. "*Squidfight!* You gotta come look!"

I sidled up to the window. Jessaloup moved aside and pushed me up closer with his nose. "Can you see it?" he said excitedly.

Oh my God.

The others sometimes teased me for being a little slow. This time, I probably set the whale record for speed. I was faster than a rocket. Faster than the speed of light. Faster than a fin whale in a hurry. In just a blink of an eye I'd made my way from the ocean floor to the surface.

Jessaloup and the babies weren't far behind me. As he came up, Jessaloup was grinning widely, very pleased with himself. "Come on," he protested, blowing a double plume of spray from his spout. "It wasn't that bad!"

But it *was* that bad, for me. It was three white human skulls, lolling in a mess of brown seaweed and barnacles.

seven

RINGING and pinging were getting easier for me. As my confidence grew, I started straying farther from the family, exploring the seabed on my own. I'd never imagined, when I lived on land, that the sea was so full of interesting things. I had always thought of the bottom as flat and empty, like a beach at low tide. Instead, I discovered a dazzling new world: towering seaweed as tall as any tree, giant seashells and squid, rainbow jellyfish glowing like stained-glass windows; mountains and valleys, canyons and cliffs, deserts and jungles, moonscapes and prairies. I knew that I was one of very few humans who would ever visit this vast underworld, and it made me glow with pride.

One day, on one of my solitary swims, I heard a sound that wasn't right. An eerie shriek pierced the water, followed by horrible moans and short bursts of warnings: *"Stay away. Danger. Do not approach. Danger."*

I tore back to where I'd left the family.

"What's that?" I panted as soon as I found Onijonah. "What's happened?"

"Stay calm, stay calm," said Onijonah. "It's Dilgruel. She is in trouble. That's her, warning us to stay away."

I now noticed that Onijonah had her flippers tightly locked around Tomturan, who was struggling ferociously. "Quiet, little one," Onijonah murmured helplessly. "Don't worry. Your mother will come back as soon as she can free herself. Stay here, Tomturan. You mustn't—"

But Tomturan gave a desperate heave and managed to slip through her flippers. He bolted up to the surface.

"What's happened?" I asked anxiously. "Where is he going?"

"Dilgruel is caught in a net, we think," panted Onijonah. "Only it's not safe for any of us to go there. And now Tomturan, the silly little fool . . ."

"Oh, but we can't just leave her—we have got to do something!" I exclaimed. Dilgruel's panicky bleats were driving me crazy.

"I'll go," a voice said.

It was Jessaloup.

"Me too," I said, before I'd had time to think it over. "I'll go too."

"You cannot," said Momboduno. "You have no idea, child, of the danger. Besides, your training is not complete."

"That's right," said Jessaloup. "You can't go." He turned to Onijonah. "Please don't ask me to take care of *her*. It's the last thing I need."

When Jessaloup said that, something in me just snapped.

I turned on him and said slowly, my voice quivering with rage, "Don't you tell me what I can and can't do, Jessaloup. I know perfectly well I'm not as strong as you, and not as fast a swimmer. *But* . . . I happen to be a human. Remember? And Dilgruel must be caught in a human net. A net *made* by humans. Has it ever occurred to you that I might know something you don't? That I might just possibly be good for something?"

Everyone stared at me in amazement. Jessaloup's mouth was open. I caught Onijonah's eye. She grinned, as if to say *Right on!*

I turned and started swimming in the direction of the terrible sound.

"Are you coming, Jessaloup? Yes or no?" I said without looking back.

We found the net before we found Dilgruel. It was a huge green grid, like a filthy spiderweb, floating on the surface high above us. All sorts of things—staring dead fish, bits of seaweed, blobs of yellow foam, a lobster, an empty soda can—were caught in it. It was a trawling net that must have worked its way loose from the trawler.

"Stop! Don't go up for air," I warned. "You'll get trapped too."

"I'm not stupid," grumbled Jessaloup. "Quick, let's find the edge of this thing, before we suffocate down here."

"See those floating things that look like little balloons?" I said.

"You mean that look like blowfish?" said Jessaloup.

"Whatever. Those are the floats. They're at the edge of the net. We should be able to surface on the other side, if we're lucky."

Sure enough, on the other side of the floats the surface was free of the net. Gratefully, we came up for air.

"I see her!" cried Jessaloup. He was spy-hopping, his head straight out of the water, so both his eyes were above the surface. "Over there, see? In the direction of the sun."

"Is she near the edge of the net, or what?" I asked anxiously.

"No, it looks like she's caught right in the middle. Oh—oh no!"

"What?"

"Tomturan's there too. I see his little spout. It looks like he's tangled up too."

I dove and started messaging to the trapped pair. "Hang on, Dilgruel. Don't move, Tomturan. Help is on the way."

Jessaloup chimed in. "Stay as quiet as you can. If you move, you'll only make it worse."

Then he turned to me. "Okay, it looks like her head and at least one flipper are caught. I think she's holding up Tomturan too. It must be taking a lot of effort for her to stay still at the surface so they both can breathe. If her tail gets caught, they'll both drown."

"I know. Oh, if only I had teeth," I muttered. "Or a knife."

"What's a knife?" Jessaloup demanded.

"It's a sharp thing humans use to cut with," I explained. "Tell me, Jessaloup, what's the sharpest thing in the sea?"

"Sharks' teeth."

"No good. Sharks are no help to us," I said.

"Coral can be pretty sharp," said Jessaloup. "I've cut myself on it before."

"Yes, but there are no reefs around here," I said.

"No, not here," he agreed.

"Okay, but how about shells?" I asked. "Shells can be sharp too. I once cut my foot on one pretty badly. Come on, let's try to find some." I headed straight down to the ocean floor.

It took me less than a minute to find a giant clamshell with a wicked-looking jagged edge. "This kind is good," I instructed Jessaloup. "You get one too."

"What are we going to do with them?" he asked as he scoured the ocean floor.

"Mmff," I said. I was trying to pick up the shell by pinching it between my jaws, but I couldn't get a good hold on it.

"Try using your flippers," he advised. "Like this." He started fanning his flippers rapidly so that a current swirled around the shell he had found and lifted it a few inches from the bottom. Then he snapped his jaws shut on it.

After a few tries, I managed to pick up my shell the same way. I jammed it between my tongue and the roof of my mouth.

Jessaloup followed me as I went up for air, and then we dove down and swam in the direction of Dilgruel's and Tomturan's pitiful cries, staying low to avoid getting caught in the net.

When we were directly underneath them, I spoke to them very calmly. "Dilgruel, Tomturan. Listen to me. It's Jessaloup and Isabel. Don't worry. It's all right. We're going to set you free."

"Oh, quick, quick," sobbed Dilgruel. "I'm so worried about Tomturan, he's got his head caught, I couldn't stop him . . ."

"Hold still, Tomturan," I said. "No kicking. Remember how we sometimes play dead?"

"Yes," he quavered.

"Well, play dead. Trick Jessaloup over there into thinking you're dead," I whispered.

"Okay," he said, a little more cheerful at the prospect of a game. "But don't tell Jessaloup!"

"I won't," I said. I brought my shell to the front edge of my mouth, keeping my jaws and tongue firmly clamped on it, and signaled to Jessaloup to watch what I was doing. Holding my flipper out to keep the net stretched taut and away from us, I started sawing at a strand of the net close to Tomturan's neck by moving my head from side to side.

Jessaloup soon got the picture and started doing the same thing on the other side.

It wasn't as easy as it looked. The net was made out of nylon rope, which was very hard to saw through. After several minutes Jessaloup grunted, "We've got to go back up for air. Now!"

We raced back to the edge of the net to gulp in some air. I was coughing up quite a bit of mucus through my blow-hole. We'd been under longer than I'd realized.

"Are you okay?" asked Jessaloup. "If this is too much for you . . ."

"I'm fine," I panted. "Lead on."

This time we made a little more headway. After sawing frantically for a few minutes, we finally managed to set Tomturan free.

"Come, little fellow!" I said. "Race ya!"

Tomturan followed me, then stopped and turned back. "Mother . . . ," he began.

"Your mother's going to follow us as soon as we get her untangled," I said.

"Don't want to go!" Tomturan wailed. "Want to stay!"

"Tomturan," said Jessaloup desperately. "We're playing hide-and-ping, and your mother's It. Now, go hide!"

"Mother?" Tomturan said.

"Yes, darling," Dilgruel said weakly. "I'm going to start counting, so quick, hide! One . . . two . . ."

Tomturan was off like a shot. I led him to the edge of the net, where we could surface for air. Then I said, "Look, over there. That's Tengapoul. See her spouting on the horizon? Go hide under her. She's the best hiding place. Because she's so big."

"Okay, but . . . ," he said.

"And ask her to sing you that song—remember?—of how she got that big white scar on her tail when she was just a little calf."

"Okay," he said happily, and sped off.

When I got back to Dilgruel, I found that Jessaloup had already made some headway with the net around her. Her flipper was now free, and she was gratefully using it to tread water, relieving the cramp in her other flipper and her tail.

"Go take a breather, Jessaloup," I ordered. He looked pretty bad to me.

"But I am almost—" he began.

"You're almost drowned," I said. "Now go!"

"All right," he said obediently.

By the time he got back there were only two more strands of rope to cut. "Hurry," I said. "She's beginning to sink."

After a few more desperate lunges, we had her free.

"She's losing consciousness," I wailed. "Dilgruel, please don't—"

"Here," said Jessaloup. "Come on the other side. Now hold up your flipper under her belly, as I am doing."

Cradling Dilgruel, who was bigger than either of us, we managed to drag her to safety beyond the edge of the net. As soon as we were safe, Jessaloup dove under her and hoisted her to the surface on his back.

"Signal to the others," he panted. "I can't hold her much longer."

But the others had already spotted us, and soon Momboduno and Onijonah were supporting Dilgruel, and Jessaloup and I could let go and stretch our aching backs.

"Is she . . . is she going to be all right?" I panted anxiously when I got my breath back. There was a nasty gash in her flesh, just below the flipper. Some blood floated in a flimsy web around the wound.

"She is spouting," said Blossamer. "Look! It is very weak, but at least she is breathing. She'll recover all right."

"What should we do about the bleeding?" I said. I was thinking Band-Aids, but of course there's no such thing in the ocean.

"Where?" asked Onijonah. When I pointed out the wound, which she hadn't noticed, she gently laid her flipper against the cut and held it there. After a minute or so she took her flipper away, and I saw that the bleeding had stopped.

Dilgruel came around not long after that. "Where is Tomturan?" were her first words.

"Mother, Mother," cried Tomturan, breaking loose from old Tengapoul, who had been clutching him tightly. "Here I am! Look at me!"

"There you are," she said weakly, allowing him to nestle under her flipper.

"Mother found me! Okay, who's It now? I know . . . Isabel's It!" he giggled.

"Not now, Tomturan," I said, catching Jessaloup's eye. "Isabel is very tired. Isabel has got to rest. Later, okay?"

"Later," agreed Tomturan reluctantly. "And Jessaloup too?"

"And Jessaloup too," said Jessaloup.

After we had saved Dilgruel and Tomturan, Jessaloup's attitude toward me changed. He still teased me a lot—maybe even more than before—but he also spent a lot more time noticing what I was doing, and less time off with his friends.

Onijonah noticed too.

"So, I see Jessaloup's been teaching you some of his tricks," she said to me one morning. We were lying at the surface, the sun hot on our backs. I could feel the pleasant warmth spreading around my body.

"Oh, yeah, I suppose," I said nonchalantly. "He showed us how to do those flips yesterday," I said. "And headstands."

"That was very nice of him," said Onijonah.

"Oh, not really," I said quickly. "He's just decided to spend more time playing with Tomturan and Delight. They are pretty cute, you've got to admit."

"Well, I must say it is the first time I've ever seen Jessaloup take such an interest in the calves. Or in someone else's training," said Onijonah, smiling.

"So?" I said. "So what?"

"Nothing," she said. "So nothing. I think it is very nice of him, that's all."

For the first time, it occurred to me that whales don't blush. And to tell you the truth, I was pretty glad they didn't.

Within a few weeks we had reached the northernmost stretch of our tribe's fishing grounds. It was now so cold that you had to ping very carefully if you didn't want to bump into any ice floes. I was very glad of my blubber and shuddered to think that if I'd been in my human form, even in a wet suit, I'd probably have frozen to death in a couple of minutes!

I felt like a tourist—I kept exclaiming over the landscape, the icy mountains, the long drawn-out days, the blinding sunlight, the walruses, the seals, the other interesting animals.

"Pests!" grumbled Momboduno as he heard me cooing over some seals that were fishing off an ice floe. "They scare the fish away."

"Oh!" I said. "But they're so cute!"

"Who's so cute?" asked Jessaloup, coming up behind us.

"Isabel thinks seals are cute," said Momboduno dryly.

"Hah! Cute!" exclaimed Jessaloup. "I tell you, if the vermin come any closer, I'm going to give their platform there a wallop with my tail and send them flying."

"Well, *I* think they're adorable," I said. "Besides, there's plenty of food for all of us."

"Oh yeah?" said Jessaloup.

"Yeah!" I said.

I should have known better. Jessaloup signaled to his friends, and all five of them started circling around me, chomping at the water and eating up everything in sight. They left me with no room to move, nothing to eat, and no way out. I was trapped.

"Jessaloup!" I yelled, as loudly as I could. "Jessaloup! Lemmertail! Trog! No fair! Let me out of here! I—I give up!"

"She surrenders," said Gilrut, grinning from eye to eye.

"She surrenders," agreed Jessaloup, and started slowing down. The others followed suit. "Okay, I guess we'll let her go. This time."

"I'll bet you secretly think seals are cute too," I muttered as they allowed me to pass.

"What was that?" Jessaloup blew, flipping onto his back.

"I bet you—eeee!" He had nipped the side of my tail with his jaw. I turned and swam like a maniac until he finally got tired of chasing me and went back to his meal.

I even came face to face with a polar bear once. But he too looked almost cuddly to me, not all that scary, even though he bared his fangs at me nastily. I just stared at him until he started splashing backward, never taking his yellow eyes off me, and then I turned and coolly went on my way. It's not that I was particularly brave; it's just that I was about five times as big as he was.

If you're a whale, there aren't too many creatures you have to be scared of. But that doesn't mean you should ever let down your guard. There are still plenty of dangers under the sea.

It was the end of a long day, and I had been following a school of herring that had led me some distance away from the pod. The purple twilight had been taking its own sweet time giving way to night, but now the sea was icy black, the stars above me pinched with cold. I realized that it had been a while since I had been in touch with Onijonah. I looked around, took some deep breaths and dove, because if I was going to find my way back by ringing, it had to be underwater, where sound travels far and clear.

I could make out the form of a whale a few lengths ahead of me. I didn't recognize it as anyone I knew. It wasn't a humpback, I could tell. But I wasn't worried; the whales we met on our travels, no matter what species, were always extremely friendly. I decided to head over there and ask for directions.

"Excuse me, Stranger," I rang out, in the polite form I had been taught, "I wonder if you might have come across some Sirens in the vicinity . . . ?"

A fluting voice answered skittishly. "I-Identify yourself."

"Oh, excuse me," I said. "My name is Isabel."

"Isabel?" the voice came back suspiciously. "What sort of name is Isab—Oh, wait a minute! Now, where did I hear that name? I'm sure I—Don't tell me. My memory isn't what it used to be. But I *know* it. It's on the tip of my tongue. Does that ever happen to you?"

"Well, sometimes I—" I began.

"So annoying! Let's see now. You are a Siren, of course, no mistaking that. No, no, please don't tell me, I almost had it. . . . Now where did it go? Yes! Of course. I knew it. I *knew* it! What did I tell you! I *did* have it. You are with Onijonah's family, aren't you? The Chosen One . . . you are the new mermaid! Heh! You thought I wouldn't remember, didn't you!"

"No," I said. "I mean, of course I thought you would . . ."

"Well, well. You see, young lady. I told you once, and I will tell you again, never underestimate your old Moonglim. He may be ancient, but he never forgets a song." Now the voice lost its peevishness and went down, formally, a couple of octaves. "Be greeted, Isabel. Have I introduced myself yet? Did I not just . . . ? Oh well. How do you do, anyway? The name is Moonglim."

"Moonglim," I repeated. "I—I am pleased to meet you. I

mean, very." I felt a little awkward, because I wasn't too fluent in this formal sort of whale talk. Also, there was something about the soundprint of his form that was confusing. I couldn't place him.

"Please excuse my rather unwelcoming conduct," the voice went on. "I am not used to strangers, you see. Well, well, well, the mermaid! Yes, yes. I regret that my brood and I could not be at your Welcoming, but we do not do well in crowds. Our nerves are not up to it, you understand. And the heat would have been too much for us, of course. I had been hoping you might stop by, however."

"Thank you," I said. I now had him in my sight, a short way ahead and a little to the left of me. He was facing away from me. He was pretty small, for a whale, and his skin was a curious leopardlike pattern, mottled gray and white. In the murky darkness he gave off an eerie reflection, like moonlight on an ice floe.

"How are you finding the harvest in our waters?" he was chatting on politely. "I myself believe there is no finer fishing than right here in our own little backyard. This is also why one travels so very little. There's no place like home, I always say. Don't you agree?" With that, he turned to face me.

I froze.

Imagine a whale with a harpoon sticking out of its forehead. A mean-looking spike half as long again as his body, staring me right in the face. Pinocchio after he's told a thousand lies. A huge spiral drill aimed right between my eyes.

"Uh," I said, backing away from him. "Well, excuse me—"

"But do not go, mermaid!" the creature exclaimed, shaking his dangerous head. His weapon was only inches from my throat. I decided not to take any chances and stayed where I was.

"I'm sorry, but I . . . please . . . I mean, the others will be wondering where I went. . . ." I was shaking inside but tried to make my voice sound normal.

"Must you go so soon?" he asked sorrowfully. "What a shame. I was hoping to prolong our acquaintance. It has been so long since I visited with a human. Eons, practically. Stay awhile, mermaid. You could sing me some of your fairy songs. Or give me an account of the sweltering tropics, if you prefer. Have you been there yet? One does like to hear how the other half lives."

"Uh . . . ," I began to stammer. "Uh . . . Excuse me, but I think . . . I don't know if you're aware of it, but there seems to be something . . . uh, stuck to . . . er, in . . . your fore-head. . . ."

"What? Oh, that!" he exclaimed. "That is nothing! It is perfectly normal. Not to worry. It's my corn."

"Corn?" I repeated.

"You have never seen one, of course. Do not worry. No need to be afraid! It belongs there. I am very careful with it, you know. I hardly ever have an accident. Except for that poor shark last week," he went on pensively, "but he was courting trouble, that one, it was hardly my fault. I tried to avoid him, but he kept coming. . . . It was not easy, I can tell you, to disentangle myself. I hate it when that happens. It is so . . . messy."

I giggled nervously. I couldn't take my eyes off the horn, or corn, or whatever it was, even though he had turned away a little, so that he was no longer waving it *right* in my face.

"You mean, you are really meant to have that . . . that thing? In your head?" I said finally.

"Meant? But of course I am meant to have it. I am a Narcorn! Have you never heard of us?"

I shook my head.

"Then you did not know it is a Great Privilege to meet a Narcorn?"

"No," I said apologetically. "I don't know. Maybe, but I don't think so."

"Well, there it is. A Great Privilege. Consider yourself a lucky mermaid. We bring good luck. Did you not know that? My, my, what *do* they teach you young ones over there on dry land these days? Most humans *used* to know that, once. Shame, shame."

"I have heard of unicorns, of course," I said quickly. I didn't want him to think I was stupid. "But Narcorns . . . I don't think so."

"Well, there you have it," he said. "It is one and the same thing, or it used to be. Unicorns, Narcorns. Only you humans now call us narwhals, or some such ridiculous name. You've completely forgotten about us, it seems."

"Forgotten about you?" I said.

"Out of sight, out of mind. Ah well," he sighed. "So it goes."

We were now spouting at the surface, and he began to scrape idly with his pick at a floating chunk of ice.

"Excuse me," I said. "But what do you mean, forgotten about you?"

"Ah well, you know," he said. "Back in the old days, your

kind made a big fuss over us. Thought we had magic properties. Worshipped us like gods, practically."

"You mean unicorns?" I said. I felt it would be neither courteous nor safe to challenge him.

"Yes, unicorns, if you like."

"But how could *you* have been a unicorn?" I asked politely. "Unicorns have four legs, and hooves, and everything."

"Not me, of course, child. My ancestors," he explained mournfully. "I could tell you about them, if you are interested."

"Okay," I said. "I'm interested."

"You were saying you had to get back . . . ?" he said.

"Well, yes, but not right away," I answered quickly. "Besides, if they miss me they can come and find me."

"Fine. Let's see now. Where shall I start? Well, I suppose you know about the unicorns. From your human songs and such."

"From fairy tales? Yes. I guess."

"Indeed. My ancestors were, at first, flattered by the attention. Humans really doted on us. They were convinced that our corns had magical properties. They could counteract poisons, cure human illnesses, and so forth. Pure young maidens—such as yourself—were sent forth to pet us. My ancestors were happy to play along a little and even performed the odd little miracle or two. But then . . ."

He shook his head sadly and sighed.

"Then . . . ?" I prompted, leaning sideways a little to avoid the shaking horn.

"The whole thing backfired on us," he said. "We should

have known better. The human race started hunting us, killing us for our corns, which they ground to powder,"—he shuddered—"and used for potions and such."

"Oh!" I said. "Oh, I'm terribly sorry. . . ."

"So you should be," he said dryly. "In the end, there were only a handful of us left. And one does get so tired of being chased and hunted. Doesn't one! Therefore it was decided we should go back to live in the sea. It had been done before, you know. Other species of whales—Sirens, too—were land animals once. Didn't you know that?"

"No, I did not," I said.

"Oh yes, oh yes. All whales, and dolphins, and the like. All once lived on land, just like you. We decided they were on to a good thing. So we entered the ocean. Up north, as far away from the human race as we could get. And here we are."

"I . . . see," I said.

"Of course you see. Of course you do! But that is not the end of it, young one," he went on. "For a while there, they left us alone. But then they started hunting us again. With harpoons this time. It is not even safe for us up here anymore. Many of us have died. Soon Narcorns too will be no more."

"That's terrible," I whispered.

"Ah well," he said. "But there it is. No place to go where one may escape one's fate."

I didn't know what to say.

"And yet," he said in his reedy voice, "and yet it is still a pleasure to meet a member of the human race. In the flesh, as it were. You do not strike me as the type to hunt unicorns."

"Oh no," I assured him. "Me? I would never—"

"No hard feelings, then. Friends?"

He stuck out his corn, and something told me that he intended for me to shake it. I held it between my two flippers. "Friends," I said.

When I got back to the pack, they were all waiting for me in silence, hovering below the surface in a large semicircle. Even old Tengapoul, who usually joined us only when there was a crisis of some sort, was there, gazing at me.

"Hi, gang!" I said. "What's going on?"

"You have been blessed, child," said Onijonah, all misty-eyed.

"Blessed?" I said. "What do you mean, blessed?"

Momboduno cleared his throat. "We ... er ... overheard your encounter with Moonglim," he said.

"You were *spying* on me?" I said accusingly.

"Spying?" he replied, puzzled. "Spying? Sound travels. Whales have no secrets from one another."

"Oh, right," I said. "Sorry, I forgot. So anyway, what's the big deal?"

"Narcorns usually stay out of our way," Onijonah explained. "We are too big for their taste. And too noisy and unruly. If you meet one, it is because he intends for you to meet him."

"And touching a Narcorn brings good luck," added Tengapoul in her deep shaky voice. "It is a very special privilege for a whale, my child."

"I know, that is what Moonglim told me," I said.

"It is a gift," said Onijonah. "A precious gift. When you touched his corn, did you see anything unusual?"

"No," I said. "I didn't see anything. Nothing real, I mean."

"But you did see something, nevertheless?"

"Well, it depends," I said.

"Something you might call not-real?"

"Yes," I said.

When I had touched Moonglim's corn, for a fleeting moment I had seen a brilliant picture, a scene of a beautiful woman, a queen, her long hair dripping wet, standing waist-deep in a sea that glittered in the sun like diamonds. She was holding up her hands and looking up at the sky, as if she was waiting to catch something precious that was drifting down to earth. Behind her, I saw a unicorn, gleaming white, pawing the bank with his hoof and tossing his silvery mane. Then the picture had faded.

"Don't tell us what you saw," said Onijonah quickly. "That is your gift."

"But what's it for?" I asked.

"Does it make you happy to think of it?"

It was true. It made me think everything was for the best. It made me happier about being a whale. It made my homesickness less intense. It made me stop worrying whether I'd ever get my human form back. It made me calm; it made me glow. "Yes," I said. "Very happy."

"Then do not doubt anymore. It has found its way to your heart. It will give you strength. It will stand you in good stead."

"But it's not real," I said.

"Narcorns are real. You saw that for yourself."

"Yes, but the picture I saw. That was only in my mind."

"It is real. How can something that is true in your heart and in your mind not be real?"

I didn't really have any answer for that.

eight

THE long days were getting shorter; it was getting colder at night; we were gradually drifting southward, and still the feeding frenzy continued. I had by now mastered the finer points of harvesting. I knew how to blow a bubble cloud from below, sending my prey sprawling up to the surface, where I could scoop it up easily. I'd also begun spinning bubble nets, although that trick was harder to learn. What you had to do was swim around your prey in circles, puffing strings of bubbles out of your blowhole. By matching your swimming speed to the tempo of your snorting, you were supposed to be able to space the bubbles in such a way that they made a kind of swirling net. If you were an expert at it, you could lasso a whole school of fish in one neat space and then swallow them in one big gulp.

No such luck for me. Most of the time I just managed to scatter my prey in all directions.

Sometimes, though, the others let me join them in group-harvest. In group-harvest, I didn't have to use my own judgment; all I had to do was follow orders. A bunch of us would circle a field of prey, Onijonah or Momboduno calling out instructions, and with precision timing, we'd spin a huge bubble net and then all plunge into the middle for the kill.

"Oh, gross!" I moaned at one of these circle feeding sessions. "Gilrut's swallowed another cormorant!"

"Gilrut the carnivore," grinned Jessaloup. "He likes birds. Hey, Gilrut!"

"Mmm?" smirked Gilrut.

"With all the feathers you've gulped down, someday you're going to sprout wings and fly away!"

Gilrut opened his mouth and belched loudly.

I was always very careful not to snap my jaws shut on any of the birds that pestered us while we were feeding. But there were some members of the family, like Gilrut, who made bird-munching a sport.

"Gilrut, can't you leave the poor birds alone?" I shouted at him.

"Look, if some pesky bird wants to peck the food right out of my mouth," snorted Gilrut, "it's his own fault. Serves him right."

"I've had enough of this," I muttered, and drifted out of the circle. I was getting tired of eating all the time. I longed for my normal routine back home—three meals a day, and maybe a snack if I got hungry. But this constant, incessant feeding—it was insane. I felt like a pig. I didn't want to be part of it anymore.

It was at times like these that I'd remind myself I was a girl, not a whale. A girl who was a long way from home.

"Come on, Isabel, eat," Onijonah said, seeing me lounging underwater.

"I'm not hungry anymore, Onijonah," I complained. "Besides, I'm getting fat."

"Fat is good," she said, "for a whale. Eat!"

"But why?" I moaned. "I feel like I'm going to burst!"

"You will not burst," she said. "You are saving up blubber for later. When we leave our feeding grounds, there will be no more harvesting. There will be no more serious eating until we return this way next year. It will be slim pickings at best. You will be glad you stocked up for winter."

"You mean we're going to starve, where we're heading?" I asked, alarmed.

"*We* will not starve, because we are stocking up. *You* might starve, if you refuse to eat now," said Onijonah. "Understand?"

"I understand," I said, and obediently started plowing through the fields of fish and shrimp again, my mouth open, my tongue pumping up and down like a reluctant piston.

Just when I was beginning to think that the feeding would never stop, and that I was going to explode if I had another mouthful, we abruptly stepped up the pace of our trek southward. All of a sudden, eating wasn't important anymore. It was as if we had a train to catch. I was glad I was now a strong enough swimmer to keep up with the pack. Hardly even stopping to sleep, we chugged on steadily, day in, day out.

"Hey! What's the big hurry?" I panted, on the second day, after many hours of hard swimming. "Aren't we ever going to stop for a rest?"

"Oh, come on!" said Onijonah. "It's not time for a rest yet. We've only just started. Come on, you can do it. You've got to do it. You are a whale now!"

"But why?" I moaned.

"We are going Home," she said.

My heart did a flip.

"You mean . . . you're taking me home?" I squeaked, my throat tight.

"Oh no, I am sorry. Don't misunderstand. We are *all* going Home—*our* Home—the Sirens' Home," she said, and she said it with such mystery and such longing that Home sounded like the most wonderful, romantic place in the world to be.

I should have known.

"Oh. Okay. So, where's this Home?" I sighed.

"Oh, far, far away. In the South. It will take us weeks to get there, so you had better keep moving."

Home.

I let myself fall behind a little. I was thinking about that word *home,* and what it meant to me, and what it could possibly mean to Onijonah, whose home was the whole wide ocean. Me, I belonged in Provincetown, in an old blue house, and in my own little room at the very top. I started wondering about things, and wondering about things made me more and more anxious, as it usually did. I wondered if my brothers had found my secret diary yet. I wondered if Molly had chosen a new best friend. I wondered if anyone had thought of feeding Esmerelda, my goldfish. I wondered if they'd had a funeral for me, and what kind of flowers there had been, and what people had said about me. I imagined Mr. Peake giving a moving eulogy about how special I was. I wondered if Mom and Dad had cried a lot when they found out I wasn't coming home. I wondered if I'd ever get to see my home again.

I was beginning to feel seriously sorry for myself when I noticed Jessaloup swimming only a few lengths in front of me. Usually he and his gang were far ahead, way out of range. There was something about the way he was swimming that made me think he wanted me to catch up with him.

"Jessaloup!" I rang out.

He turned and waited for me. "Hey! It's the Hump!" he said, as if this was a surprise. "How's the swimming going?"

"Fine," I said, unable to think of anything clever or mean to say for once. "And you?"

"Oh," he said, blowing at the surface with a loud toot, "just traveling along. You know." And then, as an afterthought, "Want to team up?"

"Sure," I said, trying not to sound too eager. "Okay."

Teaming up meant swimming together. There was no way I could have turned him down. Anyone would have been thrilled to be asked by Jessaloup, the most athletic swimmer in our pod.

After spouting at the surface to get a little extra air, we

were off. Jessaloup would leap out of the water first, and I'd follow, trying to match his jumps. He was fast, and he jumped high. But I was never too far behind. I felt powerful yet light. It was great once you got a good rhythm going—blow, leap, dive. Blow, leap, dive. The waves parted before us like rows of courtiers bowing, and the spray we sent up glittered like handfuls of jewels tossed into the air. Sometimes we would breach straight up and do half-turns in the air, landing on our backs with a loud smack. Other times we'd swim under the surface, pumping our tails up and down as hard as we could, coming up every few lengths to spout. Or, if the sea was glassy-calm, we would scoot over the top of the water, skimming the surface like a couple of gigantic dragonflies.

Later on, when I got to be more confident, I would sometimes take over the lead, daring Jessaloup to copy new moves that I made up as I went along. One really complicated one that I remember involved swimming upside down and backward, tail first. We didn't get very far that way. I don't know if that was because it was too hard to do, or because we were laughing so much.

The best was when the sea was choppy, the waves high. What a splash we made, crashing side by side into the foam! The more noise we made, the more screaming seabirds were attracted to us, copying our antics with nose-rolls and dives of their own. Sometimes we would team up with a group of traveling dolphins, who took turns riding on our bow waves and chattered away in a language that was foreign to my ears. Other times all the younger Sirens would join us and we'd form one long leaping line, pulverizing the ocean like an out-of-control roller coaster.

It was on a windy day like that that we were all summoned to a meeting by Momboduno. He had had to smack his tail loudly on the water to catch our attention over the howling of the wind.

"What's up, Mombo?" said Jessaloup when we finally caught up with the others. We'd been off playing an intricate game of leapfrog with Blossamer and Trog. Now we fell into line. "Why did you call us?"

"There's a gale coming up," Momboduno informed us. "Tengapoul can feel it in her bones. We are in for a big storm. Stay close. We don't want anyone to get lost."

"Get lost?" I repeated. "But we can always find each other by ringing, can't we?"

"Not in a storm," said Onijonah. "Soon we may not be able to hear each other. That's why it's important to stay in close contact."

I looked over at Jessaloup. His expression had instantly turned serious too. Obviously this was no joke.

"But why do we have to stay together?" I insisted. "We can all take care of ourselves, can't we?"

Onijonah motioned me aside. "Look," she said quietly. "We don't want to create a panic. But some of us have been through some pretty terrible storms. We know what can happen. And believe me, you will be glad of the company."

"What can happen?" I demanded.

"Nothing, hopefully," she answered in her infuriatingly mystifying way. "Don't worry. Just try not to lose sight of the rest of us, that's all."

The storm took its own sweet time overtaking us. At first it was just a very strong howling wind and a sky the color of granite. The air felt heavy as lead, and it was filled with spray. Swimming became harder because the waves kept getting rougher, but we were able to plod on at a steady pace, keeping in close contact with each other. Dilgruel and Feeonah each had her calf swimming in the hollow just behind her own back fin, so that the little ones were practically being pulled along in their mothers' wake and did not have to struggle so hard to keep up.

During a lull in the wind, I overheard Onijonah shout to Momboduno, "I'm worried about Mother. She had a hard time in that last storm, off the southern shore last fall, remember? This one feels like it is going to be an even bigger one."

"We are keeping an eye on her," Momboduno reassured her. "I have assigned Bickseye and Lemmertail to escort her. They are to report to me if she starts flagging."

I looked back anxiously at Tengapoul, who was swimming intently, flanked by her grandsons Bickseye and Lemmertail. She seemed to be doing all right.

Now the waves were mountains and the spaces between them deep canyons. We spent most of the time underwater, where it was calmer, but every time we came up for air we could see that things were getting a little wilder up there. Jagged lightning tore the sky apart, and the waves hissed and parted before it like dancing slaves. The wind and thunder were so loud that they hurt our ears horribly; even underwater there were booms and crashes that made it almost impossible to communicate. I tried to stay under for as long as I could, but even there I did not feel safe. The ocean was filled with disoriented fish and worms and eels and creepy-looking crablike creatures darting in a panic from here to there. It made my skin crawl, all these living things that we didn't usually see—I guess they usually hid because they were scared of us—swimming right at us, as if we weren't even there. Their eyes lit up like zombies' eyes in the flickering strobe light that pierced even the lowest depths. My companions looked like fluorescent ghosts, and the dead fish and debris spinning in the muck shone with horrible colors I had never seen before.

It was a terrible effort just to go up for air. If you tried to spout, chances were a huge hundred-ton wave would come crashing down on top of your blowhole. At one point, a wave tossed me up as if I were no heavier than a matchstick and threw me down hard, knocking the wind out of me.

For a moment I was dazed, not knowing what had hit me. Then I felt Onijonah's flipper giving me a shove, and Jessaloup on the other side of me, steadying me between them.

"Thanks, guys," I said weakly, even though there was no way they could hear me. Then I realized. Onijonah and Jessaloup were my bodyguards, the same way Bickseye and Lemmertail were assigned to escort Tengapoul. Nobody trusted me to be strong enough to fend for myself.

The funny thing was, I didn't really mind.

The storm went on for hours. Day turned into night, and still the wind screamed and the waves smashed into us with the force of concrete, and the sea shook like a liquid earthquake. I felt like I was in a boxing match with Nature. You couldn't lower your guard, not even for a second. Blindly I swam on, only vaguely aware of my protectors, somewhere close by.

Just as I thought I couldn't go on and started thinking about how nice it would be to just give up and quit fighting, the sea began to quiet down.

"Onijonah?" I called out.

"Here!" I could hear her voice over the wind. That was a good sign. It meant the wind was calming too.

"Jessaloup?"

"Right behind you."

"Oh God," I sobbed. "Is it over?"

"Soon," Onijonah shouted. "Just hang on for a little while longer."

It was another half an hour or so before it was calm enough to let down our guard. Blissfully, we wobbled at the surface, resting our exhausted muscles. My whole body felt like a wad of soggy marshmallow. I could have slept for three years. But first we had to make sure the rest of the pod was all right. Onijonah started ringing to them.

"Momboduno?"

"Over here. And Feeonah and Dilgruel and the calves are with me. All fine, a little the worse for wear, poor little things."

"Gilrut . . ."

"Present and correct. With Blossamer and Trog. Coming over."

Onijonah sighed a sigh of relief.

"Okay now. Tengapoul?"

There was no immediate answer.

"Tengapoul!" she repeated in another direction.

"She cannot hear you," came a message.

"Who is that? Lemmertail?"

"Yes."

"Where is Tengapoul? Tell me!"

"I am so sorry. She didn't make it."

"Oh, Lemmertail," said Onijonah with a sob, her white belly heaving. "She's dead?"

"She told us to save ourselves. She was too heavy for us to hold up, in the end. We couldn't do it. We tried, but she slipped out of our grasp. She is gone."

Bickseye chimed in. "The last thing she said was that she was happy that she would be remembered in the Song."

"Oh, Lemmertail. And Bickseye, too. You are fine whales. You did your best."

Everyone was stunned. Gathering my last ounce of strength, I followed Onijonah and Jessaloup in the direction of Lemmertail's signal.

I was shaking. *Tengapoul is dead,* I kept thinking. *She is gone. She won't be there to tell us stories or to get mad at us if we make too much noise. We can't use her as a hiding place for hide-and-ping anymore. If it hadn't been for the storm, she would still be with us.* "It's so unfair," I whispered.

"It may seem unfair to you. But it is not. She was old, you see," said Momboduno gently. "And very sick. She had a good long life."

Onijonah gathered everyone together. "We must find her," she said. "We must sing for her."

A party was sent out to ping for Tengapoul. It wasn't long before Dilgruel found her, lying on the sandy bottom.

We formed a circle around the body. Tengapoul's eyes were closed, and her mouth looked downturned and very sad. That was because of the way she was lying squashed flat on the ocean floor, her throat and belly hidden in the sand.

We all assumed the singing position, heads down.

The farewell song was pretty simple, simple enough for even me to understand. It said that we would miss her. It said that we would never forget her. It listed all the seasons she had been alive, all the whales who had been her companions, all the matings and breedings, the names of her children and grandchildren, all the adventures she had had. It detailed the route her family took every spring to the north, and the return trip south in the fall. It told of her ancestors, and it recorded the manner of her death.

Then the whales all began stirring up the silt around her with their heads and, using their mouths as shovels, piled mounds of sand over her huge bulk. In the end, you could hardly tell where she was buried. Where Tengapoul had been, there was now just a hill—just one of the many hills dotting the rolling ocean floor.

nine

ONE day, not long after the big storm, I spotted a couple of small boats on the horizon. "Boat!" I rang out.

Onijonah drew up next to me and poked her head out of the water.

"Oh, don't worry," she said, and started swimming on.

"Don't worry?" I said. "What do you mean?"

"I mean those are not whalers. They don't have guns. They're just whale watchers, that's all."

"Whale watchers!" I said. "Oh, can't we go take a look?"

"Isabel," she said. "I know you are curious, that you would like to go take a look at some of your own race. But it is not a good idea."

"How come?" I said.

"We don't want you getting homesick," she said.

"I won't!" I said, though of course she knew I was lying. "But I thought whales always went up to boats. My teacher said you are just as curious about us as we are about you."

"Yes, we are," sighed Onijonah. "But now isn't the time. We have no time to dillydally. We have to get Home."

"But if we just—"

"Besides," she went on. "There's really no need. We already have our Chosen One."

It took some time for this to sink in. "You mean . . . ," I said finally, "the only reason you go up to a boat is you're hoping to find the next Chosen One?"

"Well," she said slowly, "you could say that's the main reason that we do."

The water was getting warmer and greener. The colors underneath me were getting brighter. The fish no longer hid from us but swarmed around us brazenly, as if they knew feeding time was over and they didn't have to worry about being the next mouthful. Sometimes I'd poke one with my flipper, or take it in my mouth and play with it for a while, before letting it swim away unharmed.

Finally we reached the coral reefs, where great sponges pointed up at us with outstretched fingers and gauzy fans waved at us like exotic belly dancers. The fish here were decorated with neon stripes and glowing colors. Some had circles painted around their eyes like raccoons, and others had long trailing beards like goats.

"It's so beautiful here," I said. "It's like paradise."

"It *is* paradise," said Lemmertail, and Trog and Bickseye started sniggering.

I noticed there was a lot of joking and teasing going on, most of which I didn't get. There was a sense of excitement in the water, as if we were all on our way to a party or a show.

One morning when the air was steamy and the sky and the sea were practically the same greenish blue, I heard it for the first time.

"Onijonah," I gasped. "What is it?"

It was a whale song, but this time sung by only one voice. It was very far away, and faint. The haunting melody was like nothing I had ever heard. I was stunned. I couldn't go on.

Onijonah stopped too, and listened. "That," she said, "is the Siren Song. I think it is Mirgamel."

"Mirgamel?" I said.

"He is with Boonkar's tribe," she said. "We are getting close now."

"Close?" I said.

"Home," she explained.

We were silent for a while, listening to the faint notes of the song.

"The Song of Songs," Onijonah sighed.

"Well, it's lovely, anyway," I said.

"Come. Let's go. You're not really supposed to listen," she said.

"I'm not?"

"Not unless the song is meant for you," she said.

We coasted into a large bay that was ringed by beaches tufted with palm trees. It was just like those ads for vacation cruises, except that there were no girls in bikinis. The water was so clear I didn't have to do any ringing to see that the bay was packed with Sirens.

"Well, here we are," said Onijonah. "And about time, too."

I looked at her. I hadn't really noticed this before, but I saw now that she was looking tired. She had been swimming slowly, and every once in a while she'd stopped to rest. The rest of us had slowed our pace to match hers. Momboduno had been hovering near her the last few days of the trek.

"What's the matter, Onijonah?" I asked. "Aren't you feeling well?"

"Oh no, I'm fine," she said. "Just a little tired."

"Saving her energy," Momboduno explained.

"For what?" I asked. I'd thought the journey was done and we could finally relax.

"Hush," said Onijonah. "Momboduno, she is only a child."

"She is old enough to know where calves come from," said Momboduno.

My jaw dropped open. "Calves? You mean you . . . ?"

"Yes," sighed Onijonah. "My time is almost up. My little calf is almost ready to be born."

"Onijonah!" I gasped. "I had no idea!"

"Mermaid," she said. "There is much you don't know."

Momboduno started muttering something about making

preparations. "Jessaloup, Lemmertail," he said, "Go alert the aunts. We need a midwife. See if Alahoran is here yet."

Jessaloup and Lemmertail swam off.

"Thanks, Momboduno," said Onijonah weakly. "But I don't think it is time yet."

"Better to be prepared," he said.

Most of the Sirens in our bay had been at my Introduction. There were at least two hundred of them. Many came up to talk to me. They were curious about me, how I was adapting to a Siren's life, whether I liked being a whale, and so on. I was still a novelty to them—unlike Onijonah's family, who took me pretty much for granted and seemed to have forgotten that I had ever been anything but a whale.

"Tell us about your life on land," a young whale named Kressurg begged me. "Please?" About a dozen of them—mostly older calves—had gathered around me, nuzzling me and touching me with their flippers.

"Well, on land I was a girl—" I began.

"That's their female calf," explained Jessaloup, acting as my interpreter.

I smacked him with my flukes. "I can explain it myself! I don't need your help!"

"Oh, excuse me," he drawled, and swam off. But he didn't go anywhere and hung around not too far off. I knew he was listening in.

"I used to go to school," I went on. "That is a place where

groups of youngsters—calves and almost-grown humans—go for their Training."

"School!" said Nobnose, a young siren of Labdullo's tribe, "*Shrimpstorm!*"

"Yes," I said. "I guess it was pretty neat. Except if you didn't like your teacher, or if they made you do too much homework."

"What is homework?" asked Blossamer.

"Like practicing diving or pinging," I said.

"Oh. Practicing can get pretty boring," said Nobnose.

"Yes," I said.

"What else did you like about being a human?" another one asked.

"Oh, I don't know . . . there's TV, and the movies, and stuff."

They all wanted to hear about that, but it was hard to explain to them what was so special about seeing moving pictures on a screen or in a box—they couldn't understand why you would want to see pictures in a box instead of in real life.

"But these pictures tell you different stories," I said. "About exciting things that don't necessarily happen to you. It's like—it's like listening to one of your songs."

"Oh! Songs in a box!" said Nobnose, puzzled. "Well, that must be interesting."

"Sure," said some of the others, although you could tell they were not really convinced.

"Did you have a family?" asked Shelabor, a little calf about the same age as Tomturan.

"Of course," I said. "I had a father, Dad," I explained, so

they would know who I was talking about, "and a mother, Mom, and two brothers, Alexander and Jacob." It was difficult to go on. I pretended I had a piece of kelp stuck in my throat, and coughed. That helped, although my voice still sounded a little thick and blurry. "And we lived in a big house."

"What is a house?" asked Nobnose.

"A house. Well, a house is a place you live in."

"Like the ocean?"

"Not like the ocean. It's a much smaller place, and people build them out of wood, or brick, or other stuff."

"But why do you need houses?" insisted Nobnose.

I had to think about that one for a while. "Humans," I began, "humans need to be sheltered from the wind and the cold. We don't have blubber. We die if we get too cold."

"But how about the summer? What do you do with your houses when it gets warm out?"

"Er, when it's warm out we still live in houses. I guess to protect ourselves from wild animals, and other people, robbers and stuff . . . I guess," I said. "I never really thought about it."

"What is robbers?" asked Shelabor. "Are they wild animals?"

"No!" I laughed. "They are humans. They take stuff from you. Without your permission."

"What sort of stuff?" Blossamer, like the others, was confused. "What stuff do you have in your house?"

"I mean things that belong to you. Like furniture, and clothes, and jewelry, and money."

"What is the point of having all that . . . stuff if it only makes robbers want to take it from you?" Blossamer asked.

"Uh . . . ," I said. "We do need some of it. Like, we have to wear clothes, to keep warm."

"What about the rest?"

"And the rest, the things we don't really need, well, I don't know, it's stuff we want to keep," I said lamely.

"So . . . wait a minute. Can't you just defend yourselves?" asked Flagger, a young whale with pure white flukes. "What's the matter, are you too herring?" (*Herring* was their way of saying "chicken.")

I sighed. This was difficult. And thinking about home was making me homesick again.

"What's the matter with you, can't you see the surf's up?" called Jessaloup's voice across the water. "Anyone want to try it?"

My audience scattered excitedly to the far end of the bay, where huge waves were forming and crashing grandly onto a shallow reef.

Jessaloup waited up for me. "Thanks," I said when I caught up with him. "You rescued me."

"No problem," he said. "Ever been surfing?"

"Only with a Boogie board," I said, and explained what a Boogie board was. He laughed.

"I think you're going to enjoy whale surfing," he said. "Follow me!"

If you positioned yourself just right, you could get one of these big waves to just pick you up and carry you with it. Some of the more athletic whales like Gilrut and Jessaloup hopped as far out of the water as they could, riding on their tails like broncobusters at a rodeo. Beginners like me contented our-selves with bodysurfing, riding on our bellies or—this was harder—on our backs. You had to watch out, though, and do a fast backward somersault just before the waves smashed you into the reef. At first I was very cautious and only rode a little way in before diving back. But as I began to get the hang of it, I got more reckless and ventured closer and closer in.

"Isn't this great?" yelled Jessaloup when I passed him paddling out.

"Great," I shouted back. I couldn't help noticing how cool Jessaloup looked riding the waves. His lean black back glistened in the sun and his flippers were spread wide, like giant wings.

I heard a sputtered giggle behind me. "You too!" I heard.

I flipped myself over to see who it was. It was Falandrex, a girl whale whose skin was an elegant mottled black. While the others had been quizzing me earlier, she'd planted her big bulk right between Jessaloup and me.

"Excuse me?"

"You've got, you know, your eye on him, haven't you!" Falandrex said prissily. "For the Song. Well, you're not the only one. Me and my sisters, we're all rooting for Jessaloup. So you'd better watch yourself."

"I have no idea what you're talking about," I said. "We're friends, if that's what you mean."

"Suit yourself," she said, flipping sideways and spouting in my direction so that I got some of her hot steam in my eye.

I couldn't understand why all the whales seemed to be making such a big mystery of things. Ever since we'd arrived

Home, I had the feeling that everyone was whispering behind my back, leaving me out. As if I couldn't be trusted to understand what they were talking about. Every once in a while, we would hear a song—the same kind of lovely song that I had heard when we first arrived—and then Onijonah, or Momboduno, or whoever else happened to be handy, would make a point of distracting me, pointing out a tiger-striped fish, sending me on an errand, or putting me in charge of organizing games for Delight and Tomturan and the other calves. It felt like everyone was getting ready for something truly awesome, only I wasn't included.

One day we heard a big commotion out in the open sea. There were grunts and groans and I heard the slapping of tails on the water, as if someone were calling us.

I began swimming in the direction of the noise, but Momboduno headed me off. "Not that way," he barked at me. "Stay back, merchild."

"Why?" I asked anxiously. "What's happening?"

"Nothing to worry about," he assured me. "Just a little fight."

"A fight?" I had always assumed that Sirens never fought. "Who's fighting? And what for?"

"You'll find out later. Just don't go there looking for trouble," he said, and left me abruptly. I didn't know what to do. I went to find Onijonah. She was dozing, lying close to the surface in the warm water, paying no attention to the commotion of the fight.

"Come on, Onijonah, what is going on?" I pleaded with her. "Can't you tell me?"

"What, merchild?"

"You're all acting so mysterious, and it feels like something great is going on, but I don't know what it is. I thought I was supposed to learn about your ways. Isn't that the whole point of my being here? So *why* are you keeping secrets from me?"

Onijonah sighed. "I'm sorry. We have not been keeping anything from you deliberately. I was just waiting for a good opportunity to tell you."

"Well, now is a good opportunity. Please?"

"All right," she said, and slung herself over onto her back—she had told me that lying on her back sometimes relieved the pressure of the calf in her belly. "Isabel, once a year, in a whale's life—"

She was interrupted by a bellowing sound. In the distance, I could see Lemmertail spouting erratically. Onijonah saw him too.

"Lemmertail! He's been hurt!" exclaimed Onijonah.

"But . . . ," I said. But Onijonah had gone. I followed her to where Lemmertail was thrashing in the water.

"Oh, come, Lemmertail, stop screeching like a seagull," Onijonah was scolding him. "Come on, you're a big whale now. It's only a little scratch."

"Ouww," he shrieked, as Onijonah held her flippers to the wound—a cut on his nose—and held it closed.

"Why do you do that, Onijonah?" I asked, curious. She had done the same thing when Dilgruel had been hurt in the fishing net.

"I press on it and it stops the bleeding faster," she said. "Blood in the water isn't a good thing. The sharks will smell it."

"Sharks?" I asked. "Could a shark attack a whale?" I had seen all sorts of sharks on our journey, but I'd told myself not to be afraid of them, since they'd seemed so puny compared to me.

"They will, if there are enough of them and they're hungry enough," Lemmertail groaned. "And if they thought you were too hurt to fight them off."

"Oh, you're not *that* hurt," laughed Onijonah. "You don't have to worry, the sharks will leave you alone this time."

"Why were you fighting, anyway, Lemmertail?" I asked him sternly. "It's not like you to pick a fight."

Lemmertail gave me a look. "What do *you* know, mermaid? Anyway, I didn't start it. *He* challenged me."

"Padragel?" asked Onijonah knowingly.

"Padragel," Lemmertail acknowledged. "But I'm going to get him next time. Next year I'll be full-grown, and then he'd better watch out."

"One of these days, Lemmertail, you will be unbeatable," Onijonah soothed him. "There will be no stopping you."

I looked from one to the other. "Onijonah, what's the matter with you?" I finally burst out. "It sounds like you're encouraging him! Sirens shouldn't be fighting each other! One of them could have been killed!"

Lemmertail stared at me, his mouth hanging open as if a hinge were loose. Onijonah smiled grimly. "Now, Isabel. Come with me. I think it's time we had our little talk."

ten

I was so embarrassed! I hoped Lemmertail wouldn't tell the others about my little outburst—especially not Jessaloup.

What Onijonah had to tell me about Home, because I had been too thick to figure it out for myself, was that this was where the Sirens came not only to have their calves, but also to find a mate.

"When whales like Lemmertail and Padragel fight, that is the first step."

"But they're both males," I pointed out.

"That's right. They fight each other because they get jealous. Padragel is making sure that Lemmertail will not have a chance with the best females."

"Like fighting over a princess's hand," I said.

"Whales aren't too interested in hands," she said. "But I think you have the general idea."

"So now that Lemmertail has lost, does he get another chance?"

"Not this year. But there is always next year. He has another entire feeding season to make himself bigger and stronger," she said.

"Poor Lemmertail," I said. "It isn't fair."

"It is fair. It is the law of the ocean. Padragel did Lemmertail a favor today. He showed him he is not ready yet, that he has to work harder, so that someday he too will be the best."

"What if he never gets to be the best?" I asked.

"Then he will never find a mate, and he will have no offspring of his own. That too is the law of the ocean. Only the strong have a chance. Because their calves will be strong too. The ocean does not tolerate the weak."

"Poor Lemmertail," I repeated. I thought about it for a moment. "So . . . ," I said in an offhand way, "does that mean all the male cousins are going to have to fight?"

"Most of them will," said Onijonah. "Not Tomturan, he's much too young, of course. But the rest of them have been looking forward to it all year."

"But we're not allowed to watch, right?" I said.

"No," she said. "It's better if we don't."

One by one, the male cousins were challenged to their fights. Gilrut and Trog won theirs and went on to challenge other whales. We heard that Bickseye lost his and watched him for the next few days fanatically practicing his jumps and surfing technique, as if he were training for the whale Olympics. There was a lot of fluke-slapping and kidding for the victors, who swam around as if they'd just won the lottery. I kept an anxious eye on Jessaloup, who so far hadn't joined in the madness. But he wasn't in such a great mood these days.

"So when's it going to be your turn, Jessaloup?" I asked him jokingly one day. This waiting around was driving me crazy. I had heard that occasionally a whale gets really badly hurt, although up until now there had only been surface wounds. I didn't want to think of Jessaloup as a sissy, but I also didn't want him to have to fight. I was pretty confused about the whole thing, actually.

"None of your business, Hump," he growled, and steamed away from me.

"Jessaloup!" I shouted, swimming after him. "What's got into you? What's the matter?"

"Leave me alone," came his reply. "Stop bugging me."

"Oh! I'm *sorry!*" I snorted. "I didn't know I was bugging you."

"Well, you are, and so is everyone else," he muttered.

I backed off and left him alone. I decided what I needed was a nice leisurely tour around the reef, by myself. So I dove down and took a good long swim. Except that I realized, after about an hour, that even though I had been gazing around eagerly, like an enthusiastic tourist, I had no idea what it was I'd been looking at.

I wasn't having a good time anymore. I didn't know what to do with myself. I hardly ever played with Tomturan and Delight, because they had found plenty of other calves their own age. Blossamer, who used to be a lot of fun, was hanging around all day with the other young females. I joined them a few times, but they acted really lame—all they seemed to want to do was giggle and whisper and make eyes at the champion males, comparing notes and arguing about who was the handsomest.

"Blossamer has her eye on Brinklut," teased Olgineah, a slinky young Siren with curvy flukes.

"How about you! You like Padragel, I saw you following him around yesterday," said Blossamer.

"No way! I do *not* like him!" simpered Olgineah. "He's so conceited, he thinks all the females like him!"

"How about Jessaloup!" said Drabtail. "You're always laughing at his jokes."

"So? Just because he's funny," said Olgineah, "doesn't mean I like him or anything."

"It doesn't mean you *don't* like him either," Drabtail pointed out.

"We'll see. He hasn't even been in a fight yet," Olgineah retorted, waving her flipper lazily across the surface.

"Yeah, but I bet he could beat Padragel any day," said Falandrex. A sputter of assent went up all around.

I didn't like the way the conversation was going at all. "How about a game of leapfrog?" I suggested.

They all looked at me as if I had said something really

weird. "Sure," said Blossamer. "Sure, Isabel, but later, okay?" The way she said it, she could have been talking to one of the yearlings.

I hung around, not saying much, until the group broke up, but that was the last time I joined them. It just wasn't my scene.

Onijonah was nice to me, though. She didn't push me to practice my whale skills anymore. She was spending most of the time just resting, soaking up the sun, enjoying the peacefulness of the place she called Home. She was also talking to me more like a friend now than like a teacher. I tried not to show that I wasn't having such a great time, since to her, Home was obviously the best place in the world.

"Why aren't you surfing with the others?" she asked me one morning as I was running the fringes of some wide flat seaweed through my mouth. I tried to get it to go in between my baleen plates—it felt nice and clean, like flossing.

"I'm not in the mood," I sighed. "The waves aren't big enough today anyway."

"I know it must be hard for you," she said carefully, as if she had something difficult to say.

"Hard? What's hard?" I asked.

"This . . . this waiting around," she said. "When you aren't in line for the pairing, I mean."

"What do you mean, I'm not in line!" I cried. I had the feeling I wasn't going to like what came next.

"Merchild, it wouldn't be right," she went on, as if I knew exactly what she was talking about. "You must be ready for your return to the land. You cannot make any lasting attachments. Besides, you're too young."

"Too young?" I yelped.

"That's right," she said.

"I am not too young!" I said. "Blossamer is old enough!" I was only guessing.

"True," she said. "But—"

"It's not fair!" I spat out. "Blossamer is only half a year older than me!"

"Blossamer is a whale," she said. "And you, Isabel, are a mermaid."

"Right now I'm a whale, just like her."

"You are, but if you are to return to land someday, you must keep yourself intact." She sighed. "How shall I put it? Whales and humans mature at different rates. Whales are old enough to have babies at age seven. You humans must wait until you're a good deal older. If you were to find a mate amongst us now, you would belong to the ocean forever. It cannot be otherwise."

"So what!" I wailed. "It isn't fair! You can't make those decisions for me! It's *my* life, and *I* should be the one who decides what happens to it!"

"And so you shall," said Onijonah. "But first you must weigh all the consequences."

"All right," I said. What was she telling me? Was she telling me I wasn't supposed to have feelings for anyone? And suppose I did! Suppose I couldn't help it! Suppose I really liked someone? Did that mean I'd never see my family again, ever? It was unthinkable.

I was sobbing now and had to surface to get my breath back. When I was a little calmer, I returned to her side.

"All right," I said again. "Please let me have the whole

story, will you? I can't make any decisions unless I get the whole picture."

"Go on," she said.

"You know," I said.

"What?" she said.

I sighed. This was so hard. "Jessaloup," I finally made myself mumble.

"Jessaloup what?" she prodded.

"I . . . like him," I said.

"I know," she said.

"I really, *really* like him," I said.

"You do," she said. "I know."

"I don't want him to get into a fight," I said.

"If he is to find a mate, he must fight," she said calmly.

"I know," I said, "but . . ."

"Yes?" she said.

"I don't want him to fight, and I don't want him to find a mate," I wailed.

"Why is that?" she asked gently.

"Because you just told me it can't be me. He'd have to choose someone else!"

"You are jealous, Isabel."

"Maybe," I said.

"Look. Jessaloup is a Siren, merchild. He must fight; otherwise he will be seen to be a coward. If he fights, and if he wins, he will sing, because he is a Siren, and that is what Sirens do. And if he sings, a female will hear him. And if she hears him, and if she answers his song, he will, one day, father a calf. It is Jessaloup's destiny. It may hurt, merchild, but there is nothing you can do about it. Don't you see that?" she asked gently.

"I guess so," I whispered.

"You wouldn't want to stand in his way, would you?"

"No—I mean yes," I groaned. I thought of Jessaloup. I wanted to belong here so much—the whales were my family! Then I thought of my real family. I saw my mother, crying. I pictured my dad, and my brothers. My school, my teachers, and my friends. "Oh, I mean, I don't *know!*"

Less than a day later I heard the noise of another fight. The sun had just set, and in the darting dimness of twilight, I saw two black silhouettes on the horizon, thrashing and leaping.

I couldn't help overhearing them. On the water, sound travels farthest at this time of day, and they were making a great racket. I recognized the voice of Jessaloup.

My heart sank.

I don't know what made me do it, but I decided I had to go and take a look. I dove and, hugging the reef to remain unobserved, swam stealthily in the direction of the combatants. When I was close enough, I hid behind a monumental piece of coral at the entrance of a shallow lagoon.

I knew who Jessaloup's opponent was. It was Brinklut, the young male much admired by Blossamer and her friends for the intricate arrow pattern on his strong flat flukes. He was at least half a flipper length bigger than Jessaloup. He was taunting Jessaloup, panting things like "Come on, sissy! What sort of a whale are you, anyway? You can do better than that!"

I saw that Jessaloup's attempts at head-butting and flipper-slapping were pretty halfhearted, as if he wasn't really trying. Brinklut reared out of the water, twisted in the air, and landed on Jessaloup's head, whacking him hard with his back fin. I winced.

"Come on, come on, what's the matter with you?" Brinklut sneered. "Are you scared? Are you afraid the little mermaid won't like you anymore, after you lose your fight?"

That didn't go down too well with Jessaloup. In fact, it seemed to make him really mad. A blast of angry steam burst from his blowhole—Jessaloup blowing his top. I cringed. He didn't want to be teased about me, obviously. Did that mean he didn't like me anymore? Had he ever really liked me, come to think of it? Or had he just been babysitting? "Watch what you say, Brinklut," he warned, hunching his back as if he was getting ready to dive.

"What's the matter, did I hurt your feelings, loverboy?" Brinklut taunted, but he didn't have a chance to finish the sentence because suddenly Jessaloup's tail was right in front of him in a headstand position, his flukes swatting Brinklut's jaw left and right like a prizefighter jabbing at a punching bag.

"Owww!" Brinklut yelled. "Stop it!" He crashed backward, trying to get out of Jessaloup's reach.

Now Jessaloup took a flying leap and crashed headlong into Brinklut's pleated belly. I could hear Brinklut gasp as if the air had been knocked out of him.

I turned and raced away from them as fast as I could, the gruesome sound of flesh hitting flesh ringing in my ears.

eleven

I wanted to go home more than ever. I missed my mom and dad terribly. I just wanted to cry, and cry, and cry. Only, whales don't shed tears. But the feelings were the same.

"Hey! Isabel! Did you hear that Jessaloup won his fight?" Blossamer asked me breathlessly the next morning, when I returned to the bay after a long nighttime swim in the open sea.

"Did he?" I asked. "That's nice for him."

"*Nice* for him?" she said. "It's great! It's his first time. We're all going over to Half-Moon Bay in a little while, to congratulate him. Want to come?"

"No thanks," I said. "You can tell him congratulations

from me, though." I put on this big smile, but I think it must have been obvious I wasn't smiling inside. I felt pretty wiped out.

"Sure," she said.

I went to find Onijonah. She was in her usual place, lolling at the surface.

"I want to go home," I announced. "How much longer do I have to be a stupid whale?"

"Oh, hello, merchild," said Onijonah. "You what?"

"I want to go home."

"All right, but that's a bit difficult right now."

"Why?"

"You know why! Because it is not the time or the place. We are a long way away from your shores, you know."

"There are boats. There are planes. There are ways to get home," I said stubbornly.

"Those don't do you much good if you are a whale," she said.

"Oh!" I said, fuming. "I get it! You've been lying to me, haven't you? You can't fool me anymore! I'm going to be a stupid overgrown whale-blob for the rest of my life, aren't I? *Aren't I!*" I don't know why I was being so hostile. I knew she had never lied to me. I just felt like lashing out at her. I needed to blame someone.

"Of course you can change back into your human form again. But all in good time," said Onijonah calmly. "I thought you understood that."

"I don't understand anything," I sulked. "And I don't *want* to understand anything. I just want to go home."

"You *are* Home, child," she whispered.

"Not this Home—this is *your* stupid home!" I cried. "And I don't want it!"

Onijonah did not reply. She had suddenly stopped her gentle rolling and held herself very still, her eyes staring straight ahead. Her tail was stretched out tensely behind her.

"What's the matter?" I said.

Still she said nothing but rotated rigidly with the current, like a weather vane.

"Onijonah!" I begged. "Is something wrong?" I had never seen her like this.

She gave out a gasp. "Nothing . . . is . . . wrong," she coughed. "But I think it is . . . time."

"Time! Time?" I started to panic. Her calf! "What should I do? Tell me what to do!"

"Signal . . . for help," she whispered. "The midwives . . ." Suddenly her body folded on itself and sprang open again, like a jackknife.

"Help! Momboduno! Midwives! Alahoran!" I began ringing weakly.

"Your tail. Use your tail," she panted.

I rose out of the water and slapped my tail hard on the surface as I went down—the way I had been taught never to do except in case of an emergency. This was definitely an emergency.

Onijonah was now thrashing around like a windup toy, around and around in circles, chasing her tail, then bending her body the other way and boomeranging back again. "Onijonah," I begged her, "Onijonah, I'm sorry for what I said, I'm sorry, please don't be mad. . . ."

I don't think she heard me. Her eyes were staring and

wild. She was quiet for a few moments, and then the thrashing and bending began all over again. I swam around her, trying to think of another way I could be helpful. There was no sign of the others yet. I dove again, sending another loud tail-call.

Onijonah was up gasping for air. Then she sank below the surface like a stone, flukes down. I followed her, stroking her with my flippers, trying to calm her. "Onijonah . . . ," I said. "Hang on, be strong. . . ."

She arched her back again. I jumped out of the way. And then I saw the most extraordinary thing I had ever seen in all my life. Two tiny little flukes were peeking out from a slit in Onijonah's belly.

"Onijonah!" I gasped. "Oh my God. I see it. I think. It's—it's coming!"

She groaned and shook her body again, pumping her tail up and down. "Oh, look!" I cried, "it's here, it's coming!" With every push, a little more of the baby's tail became visible.

One last jackknife, and suddenly the entire little body was there, right in front of me. It was the most perfectly formed little thing, a Siren in miniature, hanging there below Onijonah's belly, looking around with its bright new eyes. I started to sob.

"Help . . . her breathe . . . ," panted Onijonah weakly.

"It's a she?" I exclaimed. My voice was shaking. "How do you know?"

"The Song," she croaked. "But hurry . . . no time . . . to lose . . ."

I realized that the calf wasn't moving and seemed to have no idea what to do.

"Come on, little one," I crooned, and nudged her with my nose. "Up, up to the surface you go, for a nice breath of air."

The baby's skin felt as soft and fresh as the inside of your cheek. When I touched her, she held herself very still, as if waiting for more. Gently I lifted her with my nose. The calf just hung there, expecting me to do something. I prodded and pushed her up to the surface. When she broke through, "Blow!" I whispered at her. "Blow, little one!"

And to my amazement, the little calf gave a puff. A perfect little plume of spray rose into the air. "You did it!" I crowed. "You can breathe!" I don't know why, but everything about her amazed me.

Now I noticed Onijonah, drifting next to us. "She can do it!" I told her excitedly, although it must have been perfectly obvious to Onijonah. "Isn't she wonderful?" I added, proud as anything, as if I was the mother, and not Onijonah.

"She is wonderful," Onijonah agreed weakly. "Thank you. Thank you, merchild."

"Oh, it was nothing," I said modestly. I still could not take my eyes off the little calf, who was beginning to wave her creased little flippers around. They were pinkly transparent, like the inside of a seashell.

"What is nothing?" came Momboduno's voice. Alahoran the midwife was right on his tail.

Onijonah turned to him. "The mermaid performed the First Breathing. You missed it. What took you so long?"

"My apologies, Onijonah," said Momboduno. "We were celebrating Jessaloup's victory. We did not hear your call at first."

"I am sorry that I missed the Birthing and the Breathing," said Alahoran, who was now cradling the little calf. "But it looks like you had a perfectly good helper."

"I did," admitted Onijonah. "Isabel has done us proud."

There was a Singing that same evening to mark the baby's birth and to record her name in the great Song. Onijonah had let me help her pick a name.

"Any suggestions?" she'd asked.

"Sure! How about . . . Molly?" I said. "I like that name."

"It has a pretty sound, but it is a bit short, for a whale," she said.

"Oh, all right." I considered for a moment. "Kristen?" I suggested.

"It is snappy, but . . ." Onijonah shrugged. "It doesn't have the right kind of song in it."

"You mean like music?" I asked.

"Yes. For a whale name, you need a little more rhythm. Now, your name, Isabel, has the right kind of song. It is still on the short side, but it has a nice little tune. *I*—sabel. *Iiiz—zabbell*. Hear it?"

"I've got it!" I exclaimed. "How about . . . Mistenbel?"

"Mistenbel!" she repeated softly. "Now, *that* is a whale name. And it will remind me of you. Mistenbel! I like it!"

I tried not to look too proud when late that day, at the Singing, the chorus intoned *"Mistenbel"* and Onijonah's baby's new name sent ripples of approval through the crowd.

And I couldn't help smiling, imagining what Molly and Kristen would say if they ever found out that there was a whale named after the three of us!

It was just then that I caught Jessaloup's eye. He wasn't smiling. He was looking at me severely. He was in his usual place in the chorus, but up until that moment he had never once glanced over in my direction, even though I was floating on the other side of Mistenbel and everyone else's eyes were on the little calf.

I felt like an idiot. He must have thought I was a total loser, smiling inanely to myself like that. I clamped my mouth shut and concentrated on the interminable Song.

"Well! That was a wonderful Singing," sighed Onijonah when the singers had finally stopped. Everyone was milling about, congratulating each other.

"So it was," agreed Alahoran. "Although it makes me sad to see how short the Song has become."

"Short!" I said. "It went on for hours! Poor little Mistenbel had a hard time keeping still all that time!"

"It used to be much longer," Alahoran informed me. "Before."

"Before what?" I asked.

"Merchild," said Onijonah, "what Alahoran means is that in the old days, there were more of us in the ocean, and so there was more to sing about."

"True," agreed Alahoran. "In the old days, we had *so*

much more to sing about. My grandmother used to tell me, in the old days, the Song would go on for days and days at a time!"

"Wait a minute," I said. "You mean, the Song is getting shorter because Sirens are dying out?"

"Dying out!" said Alahoran. "Well, yes, though I wouldn't put it that way, exactly, child. I'd rather think of it in terms of fewer of us getting born."

"It's true," I said. "I mean, I've read lots about it, and this year we studied it in school. Most large whale species are in danger of becoming extinct. But humpbacks are a protected species now."

"Protected species?" said Onijonah.

"That means nobody is supposed to kill any more hump-backs—er . . . I mean Sirens, of course, it's against the law," I explained.

"Ha!" exclaimed Alahoran. "*We* have not noticed!"

"What do you mean?" I said.

"Merchild," said Alahoran, "the harpoons are still busy, you know. Whatever your human laws may say, there are enough whale ships out there that never received the message. Or perhaps they think the law doesn't apply to them."

"The whalers know the law applies to them. Trust me," I said. "They just think they can get away with it. But they know that if they get caught, they'll go to jail. They'll get locked up in a cell—a little room—for the rest of their life," I promised.

"What a horrible fate!" exclaimed Onijonah. "I should not wish that on anyone!"

"Ha! Serves them right! But even with all the whalers

locked up, we still wouldn't be safe," Alahoran went on. "There are the nets, you can drown in those."

"Yes, but fishermen don't *mean* to catch whales in those," I said quickly. "If a whale or a dolphin gets caught, it's by accident."

"Whatever the intention, those nets are dangerous. And boats are dangerous too. Why, sometimes a whale gets slashed to shreds by a boat's tail!"

"Boat's tail?" I repeated. "Oh, you mean the propeller?"

"The propeller," she said, trying out this new word. "Propeller. That's good. Is that what you call it? Well, if you get run over by one of those, you are lucky if you survive."

"I'm sure the people on board don't realize," I said. "I'm sure they don't do it on purpose."

"Maybe they do, or maybe they don't," sniffed Alahoran. "But they *could* be more careful, don't you think? And another thing. People also dump things into the sea that don't belong here. Things that are making us sick. Whales have been dying for no reason that we can fathom, you know."

Now Momboduno took her side. "It's true. And our mothers seem to be having fewer calves, and we don't know why that is either."

"Look, what can I tell you?" I said. "I'm sorry. I wish it wasn't so. I wish I knew what to do to make it better." Somehow, since I had been with the whales, I had shoved all that business about extinction to the back of my mind, because my companions seemed so wonderful, so healthy, and so numerous. But now I saw that Mr. Peake had been right. The entire race of whales was in danger—grave danger.

Even the whales knew it.

Having Mistenbel to help look after took my mind off my troubles—most of the time. I never saw Jessaloup anymore. Every time I heard a Siren song start up somewhere in the distance, I would get very busy and make a lot of noise so I wouldn't have to hear it.

Even though the sad, lonely, left-out feeling in my chest wouldn't go away, I tried not to let it interfere with my life too much, involved as I was in helping Onijonah with Mistenbel. Together we taught her some of the things she would have to know before starting on the journey north—how to swim, how to dive, how to ping. Wherever Onijonah and Mistenbel went, I'd go with them to make sure they didn't come to any harm. How I adored that little calf! She was a happy little thing, always smiling and gurgling and waving her little flippers around, and it did me a world of good to see her getting stronger and bolder every day.

It was when she was a couple of weeks old that I first taught her to play hide-and-ping, and it soon became her favorite game. This is the way we played: first I was It, and I would hide somewhere close by, where she couldn't miss me. After finding me with great glee, slapping me all over with her flippers just to make sure it was really me, she'd go "I-i! I-i!," meaning she was It, and then she would go and hide in exactly the same place where she had just found me. If I took my time in discovering her, going, *Where's that little Mistenbel? Where is she? I can't see her anywhere!* she'd start giggling and squealing, as if she was afraid I really might not find her. In the end I would just sort of stumble over her, as if by accident, and of course I always acted *incredibly* amazed and surprised to see her.

"Children! Children!" laughed Onijonah one day. "Will you never have enough of your little game?"

"Never!" I said. "We're having too much fun, aren't we, Mistenbel?"

Mistenbel started butting my flipper with her head, meaning she was ready for another round.

"Well! I'm glad to see you're having fun, Hump," came a forlorn voice behind me.

I spun around, coming face to face with Jessaloup.

"What do you want, Jessaloup?" I said coldly before I had a chance to think. "Yes, I am having fun. Or wasn't I supposed to?"

"Hello, Onijonah," he said flatly. "And little Mistenbel. I've come to say goodbye . . . and so long."

"Already! Is it time, then?" asked Onijonah.

"I'm going on ahead. There's nothing left for me to do here. I'll see you later, I guess."

"All right, then. Goodbye, Jessaloup. Have a pleasant journey," she said.

"Goodbye, Hump," he said.

"Bye, Jessaloup," I said. Suddenly it was hard for me to breathe. It felt as if there was this huge stone pressing on my chest. Did this mean he had sung to someone and had finished his business here? I wondered who the lucky girl-whale had been. On second thought, I really, *really* didn't want to know.

"Where is he going?" I coughed as I watched him swim away.

Onijonah was shaking her head, as if there was something she didn't really approve of. When she saw me looking at her, she stopped. "Back north," she said. "Winter is over. We must all think about heading north, so we can resume feeding. We will soon run out of blubber."

"But why is he going on ahead?"

"It is the Sirens' way. We leave when we are ready. The males usually head out first."

"But then shouldn't we be going too?" I asked.

"Mothers remain as long as possible, so that our new calves will gain as much strength as they can before attempting the long journey. I think Mistenbel needs a little more time."

"We *will* be going back soon, though?" I asked.

"Isabel. I know you are anxious to return. Yes. We will leave soon."

"Oh, great," I said. "I hope so."

twelve

WE were among the last to leave. I had thought of asking if I could hitch a ride with Momboduno or Blossamer, but everyone seemed to expect me to wait for Onijonah, so I waited.

After so many months of going without food, we had all started to look a little lean and pale, and there was much lip-smacking talk about feeding techniques and the best place to go for different types of fish or krill. I tried not to act too impatient, because I didn't want to pressure Onijonah—I realized that it was a difficult enough call for her to make without my bugging her. We had to make sure that Mistenbel had the strength to undertake the journey, but if we cut it *too* close, and didn't make it back to the feeding grounds in time, we would starve to death.

The journey, when it finally came, was a sober affair. It was just Onijonah, Mistenbel, and me. We plodded along, day in, day out, mostly in silence. Onijonah seemed sad to leave the place she knew as Home. The trip was especially hard on her, since her last remaining stores of blubber had to sustain not only her but Mistenbel as well. As her calf gained weight, Onijonah seemed to be shrinking. She was growing gaunter by the day.

Since we had to save our energy, there wasn't any leaping and diving. We just swam along close to the surface, with as little fanfare as possible, allowing the waters of the Gulf Stream to pull us along.

By the time we'd been at sea for two weeks, my mind had gone totally numb. I couldn't remember anything clearly anymore—not my backyard, not my room, not the little reading light over my bed, not my school, not even leaping with Jessaloup in the waves. To make the time pass, I tried to imagine myself in one of my favorite places, but within seconds it would be back to this boring sea, with the gray water slapping at my sides, the dull ache in my muscles, and, drumming through my head, the dumb tune I had made up to make myself keep going: . . . *Breathe, spout . . . in, out . . . she pumps . . . she pulls . . . she glides . . . ! . . . Breathe, spout . . . in, out . . . she pumps . . . she pulls . . . she glides . . . ! . . . Breathe . . .*

"Alarm! *Alarm! Alarm!*" Onijonah's cry broke me out of my trance.

"What? Where?" I gasped, ringing around for her.

We had drifted pretty far away from each other. There was a mile or so between us. I messaged urgently.

"What's wrong? What's the alarm for?"

"Harpoon! Beware! Dive deep!" came the reply.

"I'm coming!" I signaled back.

"No, do not come this way! They haven't spotted you! Stay where you are! Save yourself! Dive deep!"

I risked a quick peek at the surface, and saw a boat on the horizon. A helicopter was hovering overhead. I filled my lungs with air and sounded.

"Onijonah! I'm coming!" I messaged. I was in a total panic. I swam as hard as I could, my tail roaring like a steam engine, in her direction.

Over the noise of the boat and the helicopter, I could just make out Onijonah's steady voice encouraging Mistenbel. "Steady, little one. Stay with Mama. Come on, come on. Faster now. That's it. You can do it."

I've got to get to them, I was thinking. *I've got to save them. Oh, please don't let me be too late. Oh, please, oh, please, oh, please . . .*

There was one last call from her to me. "Mermaid. Not this way. Swim away from the boat. *Away from the boat!* It is very dangerous. Do not be a fool."

I didn't deign to reply but kept steaming on toward the whaling ship.

The distance between us was shrinking, but now I could tell that Onijonah and Mistenbel were heading up toward the surface for air.

"No!" I moaned. "Don't spout, they'll see you! Stay down! They're so close!"

But of course Onijonah had no choice; there was no way they could keep going without air. Mistenbel, with her little lungs, could not stay down as long as the rest of us. The worst of it was, once they were out of air they would have to stay near the surface. A Siren needs some calm, unhurried time at the surface to take in enough air to dive deep; if you're in a panic and don't have time to spout deeply, all you can manage is short shallow dives. Once Onijonah and Mistenbel surfaced, they would be an easy target for the harpooners.

I was now directly under the whaling ship. Its dark hull eclipsed the sunlight above me, and the roar of its propeller drowned out all other sounds and made ringing difficult. Onijonah and Mistenbel were only about two hundred lengths ahead of the boat, swimming close to the surface. The whalers were closing in fast.

I looked around me desperately. What could I do? I had to save them. Somehow I had to stop the boat. I felt a scream of frustration well up in me. *Go away, go away, you criminals,* I fumed. *Leave them alone! You can't do this! I'll report you! I'll make sure you spend the rest of your lives in jail! You had better listen to me, I'm human! I am a mermaid! I am ordering you to stop! I'll . . . I'll tell on you! These are whales you're trying to kill, the finest living things on earth! One whale is worth at least a dozen of you worthless creeps, are you too thick to understand that? What right do you think you have . . . ?* I was gasping now, overcome by anger and desperation.

But nobody heard me. The shadow of the whaling ship continued moving across the ocean floor like an unstoppable force. It painted an ugly jagged trail of blackness over rocks and crevasses, sand and seaweed. I kept up with it, as if somehow, by keeping up with it, I could make it slow down. *Stop! Stop!* I was now sobbing to the shadow. *Please, please just stop . . .*

Suddenly the shadow snagged on a large object, unnaturally smooth and symmetrical. I knew at once that it was something that didn't belong here. Something told me to head down and give it a closer look.

It was a shipwreck—a small yacht, by the looks of it. It was lying on its side, half buried in sand. Its mast had snapped in two. One part was still attached to the boat; the top half lay off to the side.

I didn't have a clear plan, but I swooped down and grasped the jagged piece of mast in my jaw. Having a weapon made me feel better.

Meanwhile, I had lost precious time. The ship was now way ahead of me. I took off in hot pursuit, hampered by the unwieldy boom in my mouth.

Suddenly I had it. I knew what the mast was for. I knew what I had to do.

I came up behind the boat, in the wake of the roaring propeller, which was churning the water into a mess of spit-gray foam. Keeping myself at a respectful distance from the whirring blades, I let the mast slide through my jaw so that I was gripping it at one end. I crunched down hard so I would not lose it. My mouth tasted of creosote and splinters.

There was a space between the propeller and the hull—a space just wide enough, I figured, for me to carry out my plan. Just behind the space was a triangular blade—the rudder. If I could jam the mast in that space, I thought, it might do some pretty serious damage—to the rudder as well as the propeller.

Suddenly I froze. My whale radar was picking up something new. Something that had plopped into the water in front of the ship. Something that was tearing through the water faster than the ship, faster than a swimming whale.

"Harpoon!" I screamed.

There was no time for hesitation. I could picture the harpooner in the prow, gloating through his gunsight at those two perfect glossy backs.

With all my whale muscle, I hurled the mast forward and let go.

There was a horrible grinding, crunching noise and an explosion of splintering wood. I jumped back and flipped over myself in my haste to get out of the way. I felt a sharp pain in my side.

For a moment everything went black before my eyes. Then slowly, very slowly, the sea around me wavered back into focus.

My lungs were bursting. I had to go up for air! I surfaced.

The whaling vessel had ground to a stop. I heard the sailors on board cursing loudly.

"I had him! I almost had him! Then I lost him! What the devil happened?" the harpooner was yelling in the prow.

"Look! Over there, behind you! Another one!" came another voice. "Oh, it's his little friend. I told you we'd see another one. Let's go!"

"Can't!" came a voice from the bridge. "The engine's cut out. The rudder's not responding either. We have a problem, man."

In the time it had taken for me to overhear this exchange and a lot more cursing, I had gulped in enough air to dive deep again. I started ringing for Onijonah.

"Over here!" came her voice.

It was such a relief that I started laughing. "Onijonah!" I called joyfully. "You're alive?"

"I am alive. It was a close call, though. How in Jonah's name did you manage to stop the boat?"

"Tell you later. Mistenbel?" I called, my voice shaking.

"Mistenbel is fine also. But come on, let's get out of here!"

Suddenly I felt weak. "Onijonah?" I said.

"Mermaid?"

"I think I need a little help."

"You are hurt!" she exclaimed, racing to my side.

"Am I?" I said. I suddenly noticed the sharp pain drilling into the side of my tail.

"It is all right, merchild," she said, steadying me. "I will help you along. Just come with me."

We swam hard for about an hour, then decided it was safe to relax. There was no sign of the ship, or of the helicopter. I cradled an exhausted Mistenbel while Onijonah examined my wound.

"Is it bad?" I asked anxiously. I couldn't feel much; I seemed to have gone all numb on that side.

Onijonah was silent.

"Tell me!" I said.

"There seems to be a piece of wood lodged in your tail, like a big splinter," she informed me.

"Is that bad?" I asked.

"It is not good," she said.

"Can't you just pull it out?" I asked.

"I can, but that will increase the bleeding," she replied. "I would rather not, just now."

I was going to ask why not, and then I realized.

"Blood—sharks!" I yelped. "They'll smell the blood!"

"Please don't panic, mermaid," said Onijonah. "We are bigger, remember? Just let them try something. They'll soon see what sort of animal they are dealing with."

I glanced at our little group, Onijonah, Mistenbel, and me. I tried to tell myself that no puny shark would dare to come near such huge, fierce-looking creatures as us.

Even so, I couldn't stop myself from shaking.

thirteen

IT wasn't long before they found us.

At first there was just one, zooming above us and underneath us. Its back shone an eerie grayish blue, but its sides and its belly were a pasty yellowed white. It was about the size of a small whale calf, but there the resemblance ended. There was no way you could mistake this creature for a whale—not with its ugly pointed snout, its bared razor teeth, and the fleshy double chins on the sides of its head that were its gills. It didn't dare come too near. We were swimming in close formation, with Mistenbel in the middle. After a few minutes, the shark disappeared. I heaved a sigh of relief.

"The scout," said Onijonah.

"What do you mean, scout?" I asked anxiously.

"He will alert the others."

"The others! You think there are others?"

"I hope not," said Onijonah grimly.

About half an hour passed without any sign of sharks. We spent some time at the surface sending emergency calls, because Onijonah was sure there would be returning Sirens within hearing distance. They would come and help us if they heard our call.

"How far is hearing distance?" I asked.

"Oh, as much as a few days' swimming," she said.

What good does that do us, I thought, *if it takes them a few days to reach us? By that time we'll be shark meat.* But I kept quiet. The pain in my side was agonizing now.

Suddenly Onijonah, who had been pinging, froze.

"I can smell them," she said.

She was right. There was a strange putrid taste to the water. The taste of carrion.

"Here they come," she warned.

The next moment, a company of sharks went whizzing by, shaking their grim fangs at us. We moved in closer together. Onijonah was whispering urgent words of encouragement to Mistenbel.

Like an evil boomerang propelled by one mind, the sharks turned and came racing back at us. They were at our heels. I felt a scream starting in my belly, a different scream this time. A scream of pure terror. Because of Mistenbel, I swallowed it, although I couldn't keep my baleen plates from chattering.

"Steady!" Onijonah warned. "Don't slow down. Keep swimming!"

I felt a shark sniffing at my flukes.

Without warning, Onijonah whacked her tail from side to side like a mighty tennis racket, and sent the sharks flying in all different directions.

"Ha! You showed them, Onijonah!" I shouted. "They won't be back, will they?"

"Sharks don't usually give up that easily," said Onijonah.

The next time they attacked, they attacked from all sides. In the chaos I couldn't count how many of them there were, but I figured there were at least half a dozen behind us, half a dozen on the right and half a dozen on the left, like a pack of snarling wolves or bloodthirsty hounds. Only fiercer, more pitiless, and uglier. My heart clanged hollowly in my chest. My blood ran as cold as slush.

"Keep swimming!" panted Onijonah. "Don't pay any attention! Keep your flippers close to your sides!"

Mistenbel was still in the middle. She was obviously pretty scared but swam on pluckily, looking straight ahead, never whining or complaining.

"By Proteus," muttered Onijonah. "They are persistent, these pesky creatures!" One of them, swimming above us, was trying to nose its way between Onijonah and Mistenbel. Onijonah lashed out at it with her flipper, then hastily pulled it back in just as the shark was about to sink its deathly teeth into it.

"This is no good," I moaned. "Onijonah, we can't keep this up. They're just playing with us now. Testing us. When they figure out how tired we are, they will—"

"Merchild!" she said sternly. "I'm surprised at you! You usually have more spunk than that! Come on!"

"But—if they—if they get Mistenbel, they'll—"

"Nothing is going to happen to Mistenbel," she snapped. And then I thought I could hear her mutter to herself, "As long as I'm alive."

The sharks were getting bolder and bolder. There were now at least twenty of them. I was following Onijonah's example and kept snapping my enormous jaws at them, which seemed to scare them. But I couldn't swat them off with my tail, because my tail was numb with pain. I knew that the blood that was steadily pouring out of me was whipping them into a frenzy.

"Onijonah," I panted. "It's me they're after. Let me just lead them away from you. That way you can get away, and you can save Mistenbel."

"No!" she barked. "Stay here, mermaid. Don't give up. I forbid it."

"But—" I said.

"No buts! Don't you dare do anything foolish. Stay here next to me."

We swam on, on, straight ahead, trying to keep up the pretense that we were not afraid. The sharks hung back for a while. We did not slacken our pace. Onijonah coughed as if she wanted to say something; then she hesitated.

"Isabel. There's something I think you should know," she began.

"What?" I asked.

"Something about Jessaloup," she said.

"If it's about Jessaloup, I really don't want to know," I said. *Don't tell me,* I thought. *Don't tell me which girl-whale he picked to sing to. It hurts too much.*

"I think you'll want to know this. Perhaps I should have told you before."

I kept my jaw clenched shut.

"Jessaloup did not sing," Onijonah said.

I froze. "What do you mean, he didn't sing!"

"He did not perform the Siren Song."

"But he was in a fight—I saw it! He won!"

"He fought, yes. And he won. But he did not sing."

My head was spinning. My heart was racing.

"I see. So . . . that means . . . ," I said.

"That means Jessaloup has chosen not to become a father this year."

I couldn't speak for the longest time. I was trying to figure out what that meant. "Oh!" I finally squeaked. "I see! Well, thanks for telling me."

"I thought you ought to know," she said.

I huffed and spouted and huffed some more. Then I said, "You *could* have told me before."

"I'm sorry, merchild. But I didn't want things to get even more complicated for you."

"So why are you telling me now?"

"I thought it might keep your spirits up," she said.

The news about Jessaloup did give me a little extra energy, but that too soon ran out. I was getting seriously exhausted. I dragged myself along, with no will left in me to scare off the sharks.

I went over all the desperate scenarios I could think of. But they all led to the same conclusion. The sharks were not going away. They were waiting for the right moment to strike. And when they did strike, there was a choice. They could have just me—only me—if I acted as a decoy. Or, if I didn't have the nerve, they would eventually help themselves to all three of us. It would probably take them a while to finish off Onijonah and me. But you didn't have to be a professor of marine biology to figure out that once those fangs started snapping, Mistenbel would be mincemeat in a matter of seconds.

I knew what I had to do.

"Onijonah. I—Thanks for everything. I loved being a whale, you know—"

"No! Isabel, I command you! Help is on the way!" she exclaimed. "This is not the time to give up! Trust me!"

But I couldn't. She was just saying that to give me courage. All I knew was that she was endangering Mistenbel every minute she stayed with me.

It was now or never.

Gathering my last ounce of strength, I did a backflip and started heading in the opposite direction, by myself. I heard

Onijonah shouting after me, but I ignored her. I tensed myself for the onslaught.

The sharks couldn't believe their luck. The entire pack did a hundred-and-eighty-degree spin and came after me. Their fangs were bared in identical grins of victory. Their ice-cold eyes glittered at me, sizing me up, waiting to see what I was up to. I imagined I could see drool glistening on their crooked pointy teeth. For a few moments they hung back. Then they attacked.

I felt a sharp new pain in one of my tail flukes.

This is it, I thought. *This is the end.*

I thought of all the people I loved—Dad, Mom, Alexander, Jacob, Grandma, Mr. Peake, Kristen, Molly. And of all the whales I loved too—Onijonah, Mistenbel, Momboduno, Delight, Jessaloup.

There was a bellowing roar, and suddenly the sea all around me was filled with puffs of red blood and white shreds of flesh. *They are ripping me to pieces.* Now that death was here, I felt strangely calm. *Let them eat me alive,* I thought. *I don't care. It doesn't even hurt.*

And then I remembered Moonglim. *Moonglim's gift!* Now was the time to use it!

The picture of the lady in the sea, catching something raining down from the sky, flooded my mind with its bright warm light. I felt at peace. Suddenly I knew what that lady had her hands stretched out for. It was all around me; it was in the whales, it was in the fish, it was in the krill, it was in me, it was even in the sharks. I saw that I was just part of the picture, I was one of those trillions of flakes drifting down from the sky, or one of the zillions of specks spinning in the sea and on land, all feeding on each other, all working together to complete the picture of the world that was the Song. . . .

And then I heard a voice. Jessaloup's voice.

"Hump! Are you okay?"

It couldn't be. I was supposed to be dead.

"Isabel. Hump! Answer me!"

Dazed, I looked up at him. His jaw and the whole top of his head were smeared with blood. Behind him was Trog, peering at me anxiously. There was no sign of the sharks.

"What—happened?" I asked.

"We came just in time, I guess," said Jessaloup grimly. "You had the biggest pack of sharks swarming around you— must have been two or three dozen, wouldn't you say, Trog?"

"At least," said Trog solemnly.

"I know that," I said testily. The groggy calm was beginning to lift, and I was starting to be aware that my tail *really* hurt—worse than before. And still I could not figure out where Jessaloup had come from. "But then what happened?"

"We chased them away," said Trog excitedly. "We were already at the Feeding Grounds when we heard your calls, and we raced back here. You should have seen Jessaloup. He snapped his jaws shut on this *huge* one. A brute. Probably crushed it to death. When he let it go, it sank like a stone. When they saw that, the others turned and ran. Bunch of cowards! Lemmertail and Gilrut are still chasing them."

"Oh, you *impossible* mermaid!" scolded Onijonah, who had appeared out of the pink fog left by the battle, followed closely by Mistenbel. "I told you help was on the way, did I not? What did you have to go and do such a crazy thing for?"

"I didn't believe you," I said sheepishly. "I—I wanted to make sure you and Mistenbel got away."

"Oh, Isabel," she sighed. She shook her head and smiled. "That makes you a hero twice over in one day."

I hung my head modestly. I tried to keep the pain in my tail from spoiling the moment.

"*Twice?*" said Jessaloup.

"Twice," Onijonah said. "We had a whaler after us. They fired a harpoon at me but missed. Then, somehow—I have not found out how, yet—your friend the Hump managed to stop the boat."

"She did *what*?" Jessaloup's mouth was hanging wide open.

"She stopped the boat!" Onijonah laughed. "All by herself. Our mermaid halted a human ship!"

I laughed too, as if it was nothing. But then I groaned— I couldn't help myself—because suddenly I remembered the splintering mast and the piercing pain. I wobbled and spread out my flippers to steady myself.

"Child!" Now Onijonah was at my side, supporting me. "Come, Jessaloup, Trog. You two hold her while I examine her. It is time we did something about those wounds."

The last thing I remember hearing is Jessaloup's gasp when he saw my tail.

I must have fainted, because the next thing I knew, I was floating on the backs of Momboduno and Jessaloup. I looked around and saw Lemmertail, Blossamer, Trog, Dilgruel, and

Tomturan. In the distance were Gilrut and Bickseye, Feeonah and Delight. My whole family, reassembled.

"Where—where are we?" I asked groggily.

"We are near the place where you first joined us, child," boomed Momboduno. "Near the place *you* call home."

"Where's Onijonah?" I asked.

"Here, merchild." She was hovering behind me, with Mistenbel, and had both her flippers firmly pressed against my tail. "How are you feeling?"

"Oh, not great," I said. It was an understatement. I felt horrible. "How did you all get here so fast?"

"We heard your calls," said Momboduno. "We all came as fast as we could. You've been out cold for hours."

"I have?" I said. "That's funny. It didn't feel like hours. It felt like no time at all."

"Don't move, child," warned Onijonah. But it was too late. I had tried to turn to look around, and the pain was like a harpoon in my flesh.

When I had regained my breath, I panted, "What was that?"

"You must try not to move, Isabel," said Onijonah. "We removed the splinter from your tail. The sharks also took a bite out of one of your flukes. I am trying to stop the bleeding. But I'm afraid the whole area may get infected."

I started feeling faint again.

"Courage, Hump." It was a whisper in my ear. Suddenly I was aware of Jessaloup's firm back pressed under my side. It was all right. Jessaloup was holding me. He would not let me sink.

Then I drifted off again, into another sea, where the water was pink and the foam was shot with silver, and little fish played hide-and-seek in my yellow seaweed hair.

fourteen

SOMEHOW we had made it to the shores of New England. The long winter fast was finally broken. Since I wasn't supposed to move, I was being spoon-fed by my family. They took it in turns to swim over to me and scoop loads of newly caught fish down my gullet.

"Fresh catch of the day," Jessaloup joked. "How do you like it?"

"Very tasty," I said appreciatively.

Since I couldn't go anywhere, Jessaloup stayed by my side most of the time, and for the first time since I'd joined the pod, Jessaloup and I really had a chance to talk. We told each other things that I had never talked about with anyone, except maybe my best friend, Molly, or my mom, when I was little. It turned out we had some of the same likes and dislikes, the same hopes, the same fears. We were so similar in so many ways. I had a hard time remembering that he was a whale and I was a girl. I told him so.

"It could have been worse," he said. "I could have been a seahorse and you could have been an elephant."

"Do you think we'd still have been friends?" I asked.

"Sure. Why not!" he laughed.

He thought that if he could make me laugh, I would get better. So he told me lots of jokes and persuaded his buddies to perform silly stunts and make fools of themselves for me. They put on a show in which they all hung upright in the water and made mincing side-to-side movements with their flukes, as if they were humans walking on two legs. Gilrut had found some sea kelp, which he balanced on his head as if he had a clump of hair growing there. They all held their flippers out stiffly and nodded their great heads and waddled around below the surface like a bunch of overgrown penguins. I laughed so much that it hurt.

"You look just like people," I said weakly.

"We do?" said Gilrut, beaming. "You think we could pass for humans?"

"You'd have to go on a diet first," I said.

I was sure that with all the food and the pampering I was getting, I would soon regain my strength. But it wasn't long before it became clear that Jessaloup and I were the only ones who thought so.

There was a meeting. The great blue whale Indigoneah was called in—the Keeper of Songs. When I saw her, I realized that something serious was going on.

"Merchild," said Onijonah. "It's time to discuss our options."

"What options?" I asked. "What for?"

"Infection has set in," she said quietly.

"I know. But you've wrapped my tail in seaweed, and that makes it feel better. It really does, I promise!" I said that for Onijonah's benefit, because when she had applied the last seaweed poultice her gentle touch had made me scream, and I was worried that I had hurt her feelings. "The seaweed will take care of it, won't it?"

She hesitated. "Not exactly."

"What do you mean?"

"I don't think it's going to take care of it."

"But I'm feeling much better!" I exclaimed.

"I am glad to hear it. But your wounds aren't healing, child," she said.

I turned to Momboduno. "Mombo, what do you think? Don't I seem better to you?"

Momboduno cleared his throat. "Merchild. There are certain things we whales cannot do. We cannot heal putrefying wounds as bad as yours."

"What are you saying?" I cried. I looked around for Jessaloup. He was at my side and held out his flipper to touch mine.

"Merchild," came Indigoneah's booming voice. "If your life is to be saved . . ."

I felt Jessaloup gasp, as if someone had punched him in his throat. It was his gasp that made me realize what she was saying. "My life!" I whispered.

"Yes, I'm afraid—your life. If your life is to be saved, there is no alternative but for you to beach yourself."

"*Beach* myself!" I cried. "But I can't do that! I'll die!"

I remembered pictures I had seen, of stranded whales on a beach, drying to death, cruelly crushed by their own weight.

"You will not die, mermaid," Indigoneah said. "At least, we do not believe that you will. You are human. When you beach yourself, there is a good chance you will be restored to your human form."

"No!" cried Jessaloup. "She can't!"

"Oh, children! Don't you see?" said Onijonah. "There is no other choice!"

"No other choice?" I repeated dully.

"Once you are human again, Isabel, doctors will be able to take care of you. Human physicians have knowledge of these things. They know how to fool death. That is something we can't do. They will save your life."

My head was spinning. Here, finally, was what I'd been waiting for for so long—they were telling me I'd be going home! I'd be a girl again. An ordinary girl with brown hair, two arms and two legs. I pictured myself in a white hospital bed, with Mom and Dad sitting beside me, patting my hand. Wasn't going home what I'd been praying for? *Oh, but not now,* I thought, feeling the warmth of Jessaloup beside me. *Not now!*

"What if it doesn't work?" said Jessaloup hoarsely beside me. "What if she remains a whale? And she's stranded . . . ?"

"That is a chance we have to take."

I felt the warmth of a little head butting mine. It was Mistenbel, who had come over to cheer me up.

I cried out, "But I don't want to go back! I want to stay here! I want to stay with all of you!"

Onijonah shook her head and sighed.

"Isabel," Momboduno said sadly. "I am sorry to have to tell you this. But your only chance for survival is to return to the land. If you remain with us, you will surely die."

It was decided that Onijonah and Jessaloup would accompany me to landfall. The journey was declared too dangerous for Mistenbel, so she would stay behind, in the care of Blossamer.

"We must leave right away. There's no time to lose," said Onijonah.

The goodbyes were hard to take. One by one, the whales in my family came over to me and gave me mournful caresses. No one knew what to say. Even Mistenbel felt the sadness of the occasion.

"I-i-i?" she asked timidly, tilting her jaw sideways questioningly.

"Not now, Mistenbel," I said, giving her a big squeeze, and then another one, and another. "There! Take that! And that! And that! How I loved playing with you, my little goldfish! Don't you *dare* forget me! Okay?"

Mistenbel nuzzled my head and pressed her eye against mine, as if she was trying to look right inside my head. Onijonah had to peel her off me in the end.

Indigoneah was next. She smiled at me with her sad wise eyes.

"On behalf of our entire race," she said, "I thank you."

"Thank me? What for?" I said.

"You have more than fulfilled our expectations. The Song had foretold that a human called Isabel would come to us. And she would teach us. And that is just what you have done."

"But I didn't *do* anything!" I said. "I mean, I've learned a lot, but—"

"On the contrary," she said. "It is *we* who have learned from you. You taught us how to help ourselves. How to cut a whale loose from a net using a clamshell, for instance. That technique will surely stand us in good stead. . . ."

"And how to stop a ship in its tracks with a piece of driftwood," said Momboduno, shaking his great head admiringly.

"These are great gifts of knowledge to us, mermaid," continued Indigoneah. "Thanks to your courage, more whales may be saved in the future. Your great teachings will be recorded forever, in the Song."

I caught Onijonah's eye. "It isn't much. I wish I could have done more."

"It is a lot, child," Onijonah said softly. "It is more than we ever expected. It is enough."

"Come, mermaid," said Momboduno. "There is no time to lose."

"Wait—I have one more question." I was trying to think of something else to say, to drag the moment out longer. They seemed to be in a hurry to be rid of me. Sure—and then they could all go back to their nice little whale lives, as if this whole thing had never even happened. "So what happens now?" I burst out. "I mean, I go, like a good girl, and the next thing you know, that's it—I'm history?"

Indigoneah sent me a puzzled look.

"I mean, I'll just be a name in your Song? But what about me? What do you think that's like for me? Never to be a whale again?"

Indigoneah shook her great head. "Once a whale, *always* a whale, my child."

There was a hush. All eyes were on me. My voice was getting higher and tighter.

"So . . . but then can I come back again, when I'm healed?" I whispered.

"No human has ever returned," said Indigoneah. "When a Chosen One has left us, it has always been forever."

"But is it possible?" I asked.

"Anything is possible," she said.

We made the trip mostly in silence. I was wedged in between Onijonah and Jessaloup, so that I hardly had to move my tail at all; they were doing all the work. I tried to make myself as light as possible.

"This is the life," I tried to joke. "I could get used to this."

"Comfortable?" asked Onijonah.

"Yes, very," I said. I was trying desperately to think of something to say to make Jessaloup talk to me, but he just chugged on without a word.

Finally he broke his silence. "Land ahead," he said.

"So there is," said Onijonah. "Let us stop a minute."

The land lay flat and shimmering on the horizon, a strip of hazy purple rising from the shimmering sea.

"We'll aim for that place—you see? Over there. Where the boats are anchored. There should be people there."

"No need for you to go any further, Onijo," said Jessaloup suddenly. "You are the heaviest one of us . . . the danger of your getting stuck is the greatest."

"Oh, come," said Onijonah. "I am not worried. A little farther in will not do me any harm. Besides, I can find my way around the shallows by pinging."

"It's all right," Jessaloup insisted. "I'll take her in from here. You go back."

Onijonah looked from Jessaloup to me and back again. Finally, "I—see," she said slowly. "Well, I think it might be best if I did go back, then. You calves can manage very well on your own, I can see that."

"We can," said Jessaloup, slipping his flipper under me firmly. "Come on. Let's go."

"Wait, Jessaloup!" I said. "I have to say goodbye!"

"Sorry," Jessaloup said gruffly. "But make it quick."

"Thanks for everything, Onijonah," I whispered. She was hovering right next to me. Our blubber touched, and I felt a shudder rippling through hers. "I—I don't know what to say. I've had the . . . *best* time. And—oh, it's been great. I really . . . you know, love you. . . ."

"Goodbye, mermaid," she said, her soft eye close to mine, her flipper stroking mine. "I love you too. You have been like a daughter to me." She coughed, then turned to

Jessaloup. "And no funny business, mind you, youngblood," she said sternly, in her normal voice.

"What do you mean?" asked Jessaloup, innocently.

"No beaching yourself by accident. That would serve no purpose."

Jessaloup did not say anything.

"Remember, you belong to the ocean. You belong to the pod."

"I know," he sulked.

"I know you will do what's right," said Onijonah. I didn't say anything; I thought I had better stay out of it. "Goodbye, Isabel, dear Chosen One. Do not forget us."

"I won't," I said. "Never. Ever. Ever."

"Come," said Jessaloup, and turned me toward the shore. I could feel Onijonah's wise eyes on us as we swam away.

The sun was setting in orange ribbons, weaving in and out of a rippling checkered sea.

I took a deep breath. I had to ask him. It was now or never.

"Jessaloup," I said. "Why didn't you sing?"

"Why didn't I sing?"

"You heard me. Why didn't you?"

He seemed embarrassed. "How did you know?"

"Onijonah told me."

"I—I—Do you really want to know?" he said. I had never seen him act shy before.

"Yes," I said decisively.

He squirmed a little. "Well, I was . . ." He coughed. "It was because . . ."

"Because . . . ?"

"The elders told us that we could not sing to you, because you were a human."

"Oh."

"And I didn't *want* to sing to anyone else."

A mist swirled around my eye sockets. I felt giddy. "But then why," I said, "didn't you just tell me?"

"I would have, but you didn't exactly—you didn't act like you wanted to know. I thought you were avoiding me. You didn't even congratulate me on winning my fight. I thought you didn't like me anymore."

"I'm sorry," I said. "I thought *you*—I guess it was a misunderstanding."

"It was?"

"I did like you. I mean, I do. Very much."

"Oh," he said.

As we swam side by side, our eyes were just inches apart. Jessaloup's eye was an unblinking porthole, a window through which I could peer into the very heart of him. I felt joy, and I felt wonder. And also something that hurt worse than sadness.

In silence we swam on, and it felt like we would swim on this way forever, two silent whales steaming into a pumpkin sky.

fifteen

WE were now in shallow water, and we had to ping very carefully to avoid sandbanks.

"There's the beach," I said. "You can't come in any closer, you'll get stuck."

"I don't care," he said recklessly. "I can't leave you here alone."

"You must, Jessaloup."

"What if it doesn't work? What if you're beached, and you don't change back into a human?"

"If that happens, maybe some people will find me, and maybe they'll push me back in."

"Then they can push me back in too," he said. "I'm coming."

"Remember what Onijonah said," I whispered. "You belong to the ocean. You have to stay."

"Then you stay too," he said stubbornly. "I want you to stay."

"You know I can't," I said. "Besides, you don't really want me to."

"I don't want you to die," he said. "That is the only part that's true. The rest is rotten cuttlefish."

"So what do you expect of me?" I said.

"Nothing, I don't expect anything," he said sullenly. "I don't expect anything from anyone. I just don't care about anything anymore."

"You don't care about me?"

"I'm not supposed to, am I?"

"That's not fair," I said.

"That's the whole point," he grunted. "The whole thing isn't fair."

I didn't know if this was a fight we were having, or something else. Whatever it was, I didn't want it to end. I wanted it to go on forever.

I swallowed. "Jessaloup?" I said.

"Yes?" he said.

"But you—you won't forget me, will you?"

"Of course not, Hump," he said hoarsely. "How could I?"

There was so much more I needed to know. So many questions. But the sun had already set, and the light was fading.

"Well," I said, "I'd better get going, I guess."

He didn't move.

I turned slowly and began watching for a wave that would carry me in to shore.

"Hump . . ." he said.

"Jessaloup?" I asked, turning back.

"I wish . . . ," he said.

"So do I," I said.

"I will always . . ."

"Me too," I agreed. "And, Jessaloup?"

"Yes?" he said.

"Don't call me Hump anymore, okay?"

"Okay—*Isabel*." He grinned.

A wave picked me up, and I let myself float in, steering myself with my flippers. It was so easy. Yet I had this feeling that I was tearing myself in two and leaving a part of me behind.

I felt the harsh scraping of the beach against my pleated belly, and I skidded to a halt.

I was grounded.

The cold air felt clammy on my exposed skin, and the rough, uncomfortable sand clawed at my flesh. A merciful wave broke over me, but then it sank back again, and this time the dryness felt worse than before. As the wave retreated into the sea, the scratchy sand sucked me in deeper and deeper, as if it was determined to keep me prisoner. I tried to struggle, but it was useless. It felt like I was rolling around on a bed of barbed wire. Breathing was getting harder, not because there was no air—there was air enough all around me here—but because my lungs were being crushed against the ground. It felt as if there were a hundred sumo wrestlers sitting on my back. I couldn't move. I couldn't lift my head. I couldn't even move my flippers. I was parched. I was pinned to the beach like bait on a fishhook.

Oh God, what's happening! I'm still a whale! I'm not turning back into a girl! I thought, panic filling my belly. *I'm going to die right here!*

"Oh, look, look, it isn't a boat, it's a whale!" came a scream from somewhere above me. "It's a beached whale!"

Rescue me, I prayed silently, *rescue me, whoever you are!*

"We'll have to try to get it back in the water," said another voice—a boy's. "Come on, let's all push together."

They were three children, a little younger than me. They put their hands on my sides, and the unfamiliar heat of their touch made my drying skin twitch all over.

"It's still alive!" exclaimed one. "It's shivering!"

"Come on, come on, get back into the water," the little girl scolded me. "You can't stay here!"

They pushed, their feet braced in the sand, their backs pressed into me. But the sand held me tight.

"It's no use. We can't move it," said a boy who looked like he was her brother. "It's too heavy for us. And the tide's going out."

"Let's go for help," suggested another boy. "We can't do anything for it by ourselves."

"But it's *my* whale!" said the little girl. "I found it!"

"Don't be selfish, Cindy," said her brother. "You don't want it to die, do you?"

"Let's try to keep it wet," said the other boy, and started splashing water over me.

"I didn't bring my bucket," said Cindy. "Wait! I know!

Let's all take off our jackets, and get them wet, and cover it with them! Take off your jacket, Dan!"

I felt some wet cloths being draped over my back.

"I'm taking off my T-shirt too," said Dan.

"Me too," said the other boy. "There. Come on, you guys. We've done all we can. Now let's run back for help."

"Goodbye, whale," Cindy said to me as her brother grabbed her by the arm. "Don't die. Please? We'll be back soon, and we'll bring help," she yelled over her shoulder.

I listened to the patter of their feet on the sand until the sound died away.

I was alone again. I looked up at the stars, which were just beginning to appear in the fading sky. "Help me," I whispered to them. "Don't let me die here, alone."

But I was not alone.

I realized that I was listening to a whale song. I'd been hearing it all the time the children had been there, but I'd been too dazed to realize what it was. The sound was faint and distorted here on the beach, but I recognized instantly what it was.

It was a song. The Siren Song. It was Jessaloup's voice, and he was singing the Song . . . just for me.

There is no band, no recording, no CD, that will ever come close to the song that I heard that evening—Jessaloup's Song of Songs, the most beautiful and the most moving music in the whole world. It was a song of hope, a song of promises, a song of a lifetime. It told of the sea, and the sky, and the joy of being a whale. It told of the friendship between a whale and a mermaid, and it tried to describe that great muddle of feelings that makes you happy and sad and powerful and nervous, all at the same time. The song's notes cascaded over me and sent thrills right through me, making me forget my pain. It cradled me in a cloud of glory. It told me what I already knew: that nothing in the world would *ever* be this important again. I felt tears of wonder trickling down my cheeks.

Wait a minute. *Tears?*

Whales don't cry. Whales don't have cheeks!

I touched my cheek. My hand was trembling.

Oh my God. *My hand!* I was looking at a hand. I sat up. I saw arms. Legs. No tail. No flippers.

A wave of dizziness threw me down on my back. What had happened? Had I dreamed this whole thing?

But it was still there. The song, very faint now, but so beautiful; I could hear it ringing in my ears. For a few minutes more I just lay there, soaking up the notes, trying to pretend that everything was as it had been, that nothing had changed, and that I was still a whale, listening to Jessaloup's song.

A fiery cramp in my leg brought me to my senses. I pulled myself up again, but slowly this time. The jackets and T-shirts the children had draped over me had fallen onto the sand. I was naked. The lower half of my right leg was swollen purple, and a flap of skin was hanging loose, revealing raw, bubbly, stringy flesh. My foot was all bloody too. I almost fainted again.

Isabel, I told myself sternly, *you can't let those kids come back with a bunch of adults and find you like this. How are you ever going to explain? You have got to get out of here and get yourself to a hospital.* I grabbed one of the wet T-shirts and drew it over my head. I put one of the denim jackets over that. I tied another jacket around my waist, like a skirt. I took the last T-shirt and wrapped it carefully around my wounded leg, knotting it in place as best I could.

I got to my feet, hopping on my good leg. I turned toward the sea and waved my arms in the air. The song had ended.

"Jessaloup!" I called out.

My voice sounded thin, reedy, unnatural. Human.

"Jessaloup! Jessaloup!"

Over the sound of the breaking waves, I could hear a muffled explosion, like a messy sneeze. And I thought I could just see a double fountain of white spray against the sky—Jessaloup's proud spout sounding its final farewell.

sixteen

ALEXANDER wasn't the least bit angry about his Minolta. He said he was much too happy to have his little sister back home again. Both of my brothers started being much nicer to me during the weeks that I was in the hospital, and they've pretty much stayed that way ever since. They were obviously both shaken up by my disappearance. They've even stopped making up new names for me. I sometimes miss the way they were before, though. Too much respect can get a little boring.

Before he left for college last fall, Alexander cornered me in the kitchen.

"Come on, now, Isabel," he drawled. "Now that you won't

have me to kick around anymore, can't you just tell me the truth?"

"What truth?" I said innocently.

"You know, about what *really* happened. I mean, after you fell overboard, were you really carried away by the tides and washed up on an uninhabited island somewhere in the Atlantic Ocean?"

"Of course," I said. "What do you *think* happened?"

"And you really stayed there all summer and all winter, living off berries and fish?"

"Do you have a better explanation?"

"And you really built a raft to take you home, and the raft capsized, and you were attacked by sharks?"

"What's your point, Alex?"

"But the sharks were chased off by a bunch of *whales*? And they helped you, and then you just *happened* to get washed ashore not very far from here?"

I sighed. I knew the adults didn't believe me. They never had. But I really thought my brothers might buy my story.

Alex shook his head. "You've never been a very good liar, Lizard."

"I'm a *great* liar, Alexander."

"And what's that supposed to mean?"

"*You* figure it out," I said.

I am fourteen now, and what happened to me when I was a whale seems like a long time ago. My life has pretty much gone back to normal—except that I appreciate everything so much more. Things I used to take for granted—like living in a house, going to school, eating a peanut butter sandwich, riding in a car, reading a book, smelling flowers, watching TV, walking on my own two feet, arguing with my brothers, wrapping my arms around my parents and kissing them goodnight—the most ordinary things can strike me as so amazing!

I still have an ugly scar on my leg, but I don't limp anymore, and I can run almost as fast as I could before. The doctors said I was very lucky that my leg didn't have to be amputated. I was a hero for a while—I even had my picture in the paper. *"Girl Friday, 12, a Robinette Crusoe for today,"* was the headline. At first I thought that once I had convinced everyone I was perfectly sane, I could start telling them about my life as a whale, about being a Chosen One, the truth about mermaids and Sirens and unicorns and all the rest. But I've come to realize that it's impossible. No one will ever believe me. I did try telling my parents one time, when I was still in the hospital, and you should have seen their faces! They thought I was delirious! So then I had to see a whole army of psychologists, and convincing *them* that I wasn't crazy was a real hassle. So I've decided to keep the truth to myself for now. Maybe I'll write it all down in a book someday.

Now that I'm a bit older, I realize how very strange it must have been for my parents, to have me come back to them a whole year after I plunged into the sea. Even though everyone else immediately assumed I'd drowned, my mother and father had never been able to accept my death. "Somehow I always *knew* that someday I'd be holding you in my arms again, like this," my mom kept telling me tearfully, squeezing the life out of me in yet another giant bear hug. I heard that my dad had made a huge stink about it, making a pest of himself with the police, the school, the coast guard, and even the FBI. He and my brothers had plastered flyers with my picture on them on pylons, trees, and store windows all around our town and even as far away as Nantucket, Boston, and New York City. As long as my body hadn't washed ashore, they refused to give up. It makes me feel so guilty, thinking of them pining away for me while I was having a whale of a time out there in the ocean. And I know how painful it must be for them, too, that I can't give them a more satisfactory explanation for my disappearance. I wish there was something I could do to make it up to them! I love them so much, I did miss them terribly while I was away, and I certainly never intended to vanish from the face of the earth for a whole year. So, despite this big secret that I can't share with them, I have been making a huge effort to be more open with my parents about everything else, and I think we've grown a lot closer as a result. I realize that they're going through a hard time, with my brothers going off to college and everything. I'm their baby, and they need me to be there for them right now.

But I have to confess I also miss my *other* family—the whales. More than I can say. I think about them all the time. I've been spending a lot of time in the library, reading everything I can get my hands on about whales. There's so much scientists don't yet understand about marine mammals. I know I'll be able to help them sort some of it out someday. I've decided to become a marine biologist when I grow up.

After reading about Jonah and the whale, and Pinocchio and the whale, I went back and read *Moby Dick* again, and this time, instead of reading it as a story about a mad captain and a mad whale, I read all the descriptive parts in between. I'd skipped those the first time. This time around I read every word, and Melville sure knew a thing or two about whales! Then I read a biography about Melville's life. Did you know that when he was twenty-two years old, Herman Melville went AWOL from his ship in the South Seas and . . . disappeared? He went missing for several months— after living among cannibals. At least, that's the story he told everybody when he returned home. Later he wrote *Moby Dick*.

As I was reading about Melville, I tried to remember all the names of the Chosen Ones in the Song. Then it came to me. Guess what one of the names was? *Mermanmelvil!* Herman Melville, get it? Don't you see . . . Melville must have been one of the Chosen Ones! When he got back home, he tried to teach humans about the whales by writing a book about them. He did a pretty good job, too. And now it's my turn.

Molly is still my best friend, and Kristen, too, but we don't see that much of each other anymore, because we're hanging out more with boys these days. My boyfriend's name is Tom. He's been helping me with this project that is taking up most of our spare time. We have started a KIDS-FOR-WHALES club in our school, which we hope will catch on in other schools, and maybe one day it will be a worldwide organization. The idea is to teach kids all about whales, and the need to do something about pollution, commercial whaling, and other dangers. We put together this sheet of whale facts, and we're sending it to the other schools, our mayor, our congressman, our senator, the vice president, the first lady, the president, and other world leaders. We hope that if the message comes from kids and not grown-ups, then maybe someone will listen.

The thing I like to do best, though, is go to the beach by myself. I climb out to the very last rock on the jetty, with a pair of binoculars and my book. I can sit there for hours, just staring out at the sea. I get teased about it a lot, but I don't mind. My friends don't understand. They don't know that sometimes I think I can see, in the far, far distance, a plume of spray in the air. Or that at certain times of the year, when the waves are calm and the gulls keep quiet, I think I can hear a Siren song.

It doesn't matter if it's real or not. It doesn't really make any difference, in the end. Because—if you want to know the truth—I *know* that someday it's going to be me out there again.

And this time, I may even stay for good.

I grow old . . . I grow old . . .
I shall wear the bottoms of my trousers rolled.

Shall I part my hair behind? Do I dare to eat a peach?
I shall wear white flannel trousers, and walk upon
   the beach.
I have heard the mermaids singing, each to each.

I do not think that they will sing to me.

I have seen them riding seaward on the waves
Combing the white hair of the waves blown back
When the wind blows the water white and black.

We have lingered in the chambers of the sea
By sea-girls wreathed with seaweed red and brown
Till human voices wake us, and we drown.

> From *The Love Song of J. Alfred Prufrock*
> by T. S. ELIOT

"There is at least moderately convincing evidence that there is another class of intelligent beings on earth besides ourselves. They have behaved benignly and in many cases affectionately towards us. We have systematically slaughtered them. . . . Though the search for extraterrestrial intelligence may take a very long time, we could not do better than to start with a program of rehumanization by making friends with the whales and the dolphins."

From *The Cosmic Connection*
by CARL SAGAN

Narwhal

Human
Diver

Beluga

Sperm Whale

Humpback Whale

Blue Whale

Orca

afterword

ONCE upon a time, humpback whales were numerous in all the world's oceans. But intensive whaling, especially in the nineteenth century and the first half of the twentieth century, reduced the population to a fraction of its original size. The humpback's relatively slow cruising speed (three to six miles per hour), its friendliness, and its tendency to stay close to shore all made it an easy target. The humpback has now been designated a protected species, but illegal hunting still goes on in some parts of the world. Other threats to the species' survival are hazards from fishing nets and ships' propellers, pollution, and loss of habitat, since its breeding grounds, the warm shallow waters off the islands of the tropics, are now increasingly popular with humans in search of the sun.

In spite of all this, the humpback whale (so called because of the way it bends its back as it dives) is not shy. Its curiosity and exuberant antics make it the species of whale you'll be most likely to observe on a whale watch. Herman Melville, the author of *Moby Dick*, called the humpbacks "the most gamesome and lighthearted" of the whales. Scientists believe that the humpbacks' athletic behavior—breaching, lunging, and slapping the water with their tails or long fins—may be their way of communicating with each other. But anyone who has observed them at play will tell you that it looks as if they're expressing the sheer joy of being alive.

The average life span of the humpback whale is pretty much the same as ours—sixty to ninety years—but it reaches sexual maturity around age seven. A female will give birth to a calf about every other year. When the calf is young, the calf and its mother are often accompanied by a male or a young female acting as escort. A calf measures twelve to fourteen feet in length at birth; adults may reach a length of fifty feet. Individual humpback whales are easy to identify by the distinctive patterns of their flukes—no two whales are exactly alike.

The humpback whale is a social creature. It travels in small groups, or pods, from its feeding grounds in the cold waters off Greenland or Alaska (or, in the case of humpbacks living in the Southern Hemisphere, Antarctica) to its breeding grounds near the equator. Groups of more than a hundred humpbacks have been observed feeding off the coast of Newfoundland. Because the humpback is toothless, its diet consists of small fish, crustaceans, krill, and plankton. Sometimes pods will join forces at feeding time, forming ingenious "bubble circles" to round up their prey, like ranch hands rounding up the herd. When mating season arrives, however, the males become less friendly as they compete for the females' attention. A whale duel is a spectacular sight and often leaves the contestants bruised and bleeding.

But what really sets the humpback apart from other species of whales is its song. Only the males sing, primarily during the mating season. To sing, the whale assumes a head-down position, its body at a forty-five degree angle. The humpback whale's song is the longest and most complicated in the animal kingdom—more sophisticated than any bird's song. Composed of moaning, chirping, squealing, and roaring sounds strung together in a very specific pattern lasting between six and thirty minutes, it is often repeated and can go on for hours at a time, interrupted only by short breaks when the whale has to rise to the surface to take a breath. The sound can travel as far as six miles underwater, and scientists think that it is yet another means of whale communication. But no one has yet been able to explain why each group of humpbacks has its own distinct song, and why it changes subtly from season to season—yet is completely different from the songs sung by humpbacks in another part of the ocean.

A number of recordings have been made of the humpback whale's singing, and some musicians have even incorporated it into their own compositions. To the human ear, it's a weird, eerie sound at first, but if you listen closely, you will be swept away by the plaintive tones, and you may even be able to make out, in those bursts of dreamlike sounds, a mysterious, spellbinding story.

ABOUT THE AUTHOR

Hester Velmans was born in Amsterdam and lived in five different countries when she was growing up. A writer and award-winning translator, she now lives in New York with her husband and two children.